Atlanta's Most Eligible Bachelor III

MIA MAE LYNNE

a "Southern Men Don't Fall in Love" novel

Published by: Book & Spirit, LLC

Cover Credit: Lex Hupertz

Edited by: Lex Hupertz

ISBN-13: 978-1943651146
ISBN-10: 1943651140

DEDICATION

To the almighty God of Love and Light

"Please bless this book so all readers can enjoy in the manner in which the angels and spirit guides have intended."

To my parents Johnnie Mae Parker (May 1, 1937 – April 23, 2013) and Carl Parker (April 5, 1929 – February 25, 2009)

"The lessons you gave me will follow me through eternity."

To my sons: Carlos and Marcus

"Follow your dreams and the rewards will be beyond anything you can ever imagine."

To my friend, Linda Smithers

"Diamonds are a girl's best friend. Your encouragement and guidance has helped me overcome seemingly impossible obstacles just by being you. You are truly my diamond."

To my friend, Melissa Montgomery

"I admire how you handle any disastrous situation with the grace and poise of the southern belle that you are. You have a gifted ability to capture the lighter side of life and spread sunshine to those who are fortunate to get to know you."

For Noel Marion, my first complete series reader

"Thank you for believing in me and taking the time to inspire me to reach for more."

For my best friend Dolphis Sloan (June 9, 1965 – February 14, 1998)

"As my big brother, you took me under your wing in my teen years and encouraged me to follow your lead in going to the University of Akron. You are a genuinely kind free spirit and even after all these years, you are still dearly missed."

ACKNOWLEDGEMENTS

"For all others who have graciously given their time to support me through the writing process, I humbly express my thanks" – Mia Mae Lynne

Kim, Dawn, Kelli & Marcella
Earth Family

Lex Hupertz
Tiffani Keaton
Mandy Varley
Nicole Westbrook
Nicole Zavodny

My Tribe

LIGHT WORKERS

"Light workers are those who are brought to earth and are unselfishly dedicated to giving their time to shine their light on humanity and make the world a better place." – Mia Mae Lynne

Debi J. Fellows
Spirals of Spirit, Painesville, Ohio

Effie Kapodistrias
Effie's Divine Celebration, Oakville, ON

Nicole Westbrook
Inner Fyre, Mentor, Ohio

Chapter 1

"I don't want kids now. Besides that, we both have a long time before we get out of medical school."

Doug took a sip of his coffee while sitting at the Atlanta Coffee house. Across the table was a disappointed Tiffany.

"I thought we agreed to start a family early so we could retire together young." Tiffany jerked the coffee out of Doug's hand and it startled him. "I want your full attention and commitment."

Doug's eyes looked past Tiffany's dark brown hair to avoid the disappointment in her eyes. He stared at the picture of downtown Atlanta on the wall wishing that he were escaping this conversation. She was a very challenging woman to argue with and she usually won and was mostly right.

"Doug!" she shouted bringing him back to his senses. "Are you listening to me?"

"I am." He was now staring into her eyes. She pushed her chair back from the table and stood.

"I don't have time for this. I have a term paper to finish. Tell your parents to pick me up at two and we'll come get you for dinner."

Tiffany slung her bag over her shoulders and marched out of the coffee shop. Doug rose to run after her but somehow could not move from his place. She walked out of the door and out of his life forever…

"Aaaah"

It was 3:00 a.m. when he woke up and realized he was in his Aunt Mona's guestroom. Surveying his surroundings, he looked at his phone.

Lisa.

Wedding

Today

Call her?

He looked at the clock again. No, don't call. She should be resting. *Baby needs rest but this will be a big day. Must get back to sleep.*

***

A few hours later with it still being dark, Doug rolled over to look at the alarm clock. It was 7:00 a.m.

"What! I've got to get up now."

He jumped out of the bed and turned on the shower. He picked up the almond milk bar of soap that his Aunt Mona left in the bathroom for him last night. He looked at himself in the mirror. The dream last night bothered him. Why remember this now? He was marrying Lisa and it was time to move on.

There was enough steam in the bathroom for him to step into the shower. Running his fingers through his sandy blonde hair, he massaged his head to relieve the stress he felt coming. He replayed his last conversation with Tiffany over again in his head. What would she think now that he was finally getting married and starting a family?

After getting dressed, Doug went to the kitchen and rummaged through the refrigerator. He pulled out a few eggs and other ingredients to start a small Southern style breakfast.

"Good morning," Aunt Mona said. "I smell coffee. She walked to the counter, picked up her Atlanta Falcons black mug and placed it next to the coffeemaker. She turned her back to the counter to give her nephew a hug.

Doug embraced her. "Good morning. Would you like some breakfast?"

Mona rubbed her eyes and tried to stifle a yawn. "You're up early today." She poured the coffee and took it to the table.

"Today is the wedding. I have a lot to do." Doug said as he prepared biscuits, sausage, bacon, eggs, grits and assorted fruits. He had several juices on the table.

Mona reached for the cream and sugar in the middle of the table. He hovered over the stove stirring the grits and leaned over to check the biscuits in the oven.

Perfection!

The light tan and white colored biscuits were ready. He pulled them out of the oven and slipped them in a wicker basket laced with a white linen napkin. He whirled around the kitchen grabbing several dishes to serve the rest of breakfast. Mona laughed at her nephew's energy.

"You have a large breakfast prepared. Do you need my help?" She asked and took a sip of coffee.

"I have everything under control." He grabbed a stick of butter from the fridge and placed it in front of her. "Excuse me for a moment. I have to make a few calls. I'll be right back to eat with you." He walked into the living room to make his calls.

He glanced at his watch and dialed his lovely bride. Terri answered the phone.

"Bader residence."

"Hi Terri. Can I speak to Lisa?"

"No sir. It's bad luck to speak to her. We'll see you at the wedding."

"You can't be serious. I thought it was you can't see the bride before the wedding not talk to her."

"Doug, I'm not taking any chances. Bye."
Click

"What" Doug held the phone in his hand and was surprised at how abrupt the conversation ended. He was getting married today and his bride was unavailable.

"Your food's getting cold." Aunt Mona shouted from the kitchen.

"I'll be there in a minute. I have to call Greg," he yelled back.

He plopped on the soft brown leather couch and called Greg. Ten minutes later, he was still conversing with Greg. "And don't forget to give me the ring."

Greg laughed. "I won't. You can have your circle of bondage. I wish you well with it. I'll see you soon."

"You will. I hear my aunt calling me again, Bye."

Doug returned to the kitchen and sat across from his aunt.

"You're right. My food is cold"

He got up and put his food in the microwave. "I've got to make sure the tux is returned even though Greg said he'd handle that. I would feel better doing it myself. And you're stopping by the house to check on it while we're gone. I left a check for the housekeeper—"

Beep, Beep, Beep

He pulled his plate out of the microwave and sat down. With fork in hand, he sectioned off a small piece of egg and held it in front of his face.

"Douglas, stop. You haven't taken a single bite of your breakfast yet. Calm down. You should put something in your stomach. Eat, please."

Into his mouth went the morsel of egg followed by a bite of biscuit. "Aunt Mona I—"

"Eat. Please." Mona took a sip of coffee and finished her last piece of sausage. He scooped a tablespoon of apple butter and smeared it on his biscuit.

She rose to clear the table.

Doug stood with her.

"Sit down and finish your breakfast!" She waved him away. She took the juices from the table and put them in the refrigerator. He inhaled the rest of the eggs and gulped a big sip of orange juice.

"Slow down!" she demanded. "I don't want you to have indigestion. You've got a long day ahead of you."

"I can't. There's too much to do." He nibbled on his biscuit and picked up the sausage. He reached for the paper at the end of the table, looked at it then put it back down. "No time for that."

"What time are you leaving?" Mona asked. Suds were forming in the dishpan of water and she was dropping in silverware to soak.

"In thirty minutes."

***

"I can't be late. Lisa's waiting on me."

Rushing out to his car, he stopped and smiled.

White streamers and paper flowers covered his cobalt blue Mercedes. "Just Married" was inscribed in white on the hood of the car.

"Thank you, Aunt Mona." He laughed. "You did a great job decorating my car."

Throwing the duffel bag and suitcase in the back seat, he drove to the country club. The twenty-minute drive was a blur.

The wedding planner, Jonah greeted him as he walked inside the building.

"Hi Doug, the Payton room is reserved for you to change into your tux. This way please."

The Payton room was a short distance from dining hall. The door had a slot with a nameplate that stated, "Reserved for Bader Wedding – Groom's Room."

"I'll be back to signal you once the wedding starts."

"Thank you, Jonah." Doug nodded and continued to stare at the sign.

Bader Wedding

"I'm getting married."

The words seemed to echo throughout the hallway, bouncing off the door in front of him, nearly knocking him off his feet.

The reality hit him in that moment.

Atlanta's Most Eligible Bachelor was getting married, bachelor no more. He snorted. Married to Mrs. Lisa Bader, Lisa Dunbar no more.

Doug walked into the Payton room. The full-length mirror caught his attention. Looking at his reflection, he wiped his hand over his clean-shaven face. Staring at his tuxedo reminded him that this was one of the most important days in his life.

"I can do this. I'm ready." He smiled and winked at himself. "She's lucky to have me."

"She is," boomed a voice from the other side of the room.

It was Greg with an outstretched arm and his tuxedo draped across the other, he raised his hand for a high five in which Doug reciprocated with a hard slap.

"Congratulations, Sellout!" joked Greg.

Doug smiled and his blue eyes sparkled with mischief. "Thank you and you're next."

"No way!" Greg waved his hand quickly in denial. "You're lucky that you're my best friend. I avoid weddings like the plague."

"So did I, but here I am. Here you are."

"You drank the Kool-Aid, not me."

"I did." Doug grinned. "Best decision of my life."

Chapter 2

Lisa stretched out in her warm and cozy bed, looking around the room for her absent fiancé.

He wasn't there.

Because this was the day.

The Day.

Not just another day with Doug, but also their wedding day.

The cold spot on the other side of the bed was a startling reminder that the next time they sleep in this bed they will be husband and wife.

Knock, Knock, Knock

"Are you up yet? We have to leave in an hour."

She sighed and answered her sister Terri, "Yes, I'm getting dressed now."

Rolling out of bed, she brushed her hand against her hardened abdomen and felt the flutter of the baby she was having in about five months.

The arrogant attorney that she'd turned down for a date now will be her husband and father of her child.

"So much to do." She said and headed to the bathroom for her shower.

The baby kept her up part of the night with frequent trips to the bathroom.

She missed having Doug next to her to help her get back to sleep each time she got up. He'd rub her stomach and hold her hand. It comforted her.

She finished her shower and whisked around the room to collect any last-minute belongings before heading out the door with her sister.

She bounced down the stairs into the kitchen and saw her suitcase by the door. Reaching for the suitcase to put it in the car, Terri entered the kitchen and waved her away.

"You're pregnant. Let me get that. Mom has the dress and she's bringing it to Dupree. Get something to eat while I finish packing the car."

The baby must be fed.

"The baby must be fed." Lisa said mocking her missing groom.

What do I eat? Her over achiever groom plastered a full breakfast menu on the side of the fridge. She quickly scanned the menu for the best option.

"Oatmeal!"

She heated up instant oatmeal in the microwave. She paced the kitchen, taking large bites at a time, inhaling the smell of the brown sugar wafting around her.

Her thoughts drifted to the day she met Doug. He was with some friends when he purposely left the table to ask her out. With his sandy blonde hair, sparking blue eyes and his best Southern manners, he asked her out and much to his surprise, she turned him down.

He got the last laugh when he appeared everywhere she was. She couldn't get rid of this man no matter where she went. While taking the last bite of oatmeal, she smiled. Who knew that they would be together?

"Lisa! Finish your breakfast and let's go. You'll be late to your own wedding."

She rinsed out her dish and put it in the sink. Grabbing her belongings, she rushed out the door and hopped in the car with her sister.

Terri sat behind the steering wheel with the motor running. She was looking in the mirror in the visor. She pushed the visor up when Lisa sat down. "Well blushing bride. Are you ready to go?"

Lisa smiled. "I am."

The ride was silent to Dupree Country Club.

She glanced over at Terri and noticed the grim look on her sister's face. "What's wrong, Terri?"

Terri drew in a dep breath. "Did you know that Doug called first thing this morning?"

"So? He's always calling to check up on me. That's nothing new." Lisa chuckled. "You didn't tell me though." She frowned and her sister put the blinker on, refusing to look at Lisa.

Terri's fingers tightened on the steering wheel. "It's bad luck to talk to the bride before the wedding. I thought you knew that."

"It's see the bride, sis. We both know that. What's going on?"

"I don't know if you've noticed, but Doug has a possessive and controlling nature. Please watch him carefully. I don't want to see you hurt."

"Terri!"

"He showed up to the bridal shower. If I hadn't sworn everyone to secrecy, he would have shown up to the bachelorette party too! What are you getting yourself into? He's like a stalker or something!" Terri's face was flush with frustration.

"Stop it!" Lisa crossed her arms and glared at her sister. "That's enough. You have absolutely no place to judge me or my relationship with Doug while yours is so messed up with Ricky. I don't want to hear another word. Doug and I discussed the bridal shower. It's fine. I love him. We're getting married today. I don't want to talk about this anymore." She looked forward, refusing to acknowledge her sister and the hurtful words Terri said, even knowing they were said with love.

She stared out of the windshield while trying to cool her temper.

"I just wanted you to know I'm worried. He's everywhere. He doesn't let you out of his sight. You could be marrying a serial killer."

Lisa shouted angrily, "Stop it, Terri! That's nuts. He's saner than that husband of yours. You and I both know that Ricky is an asshole to everybody. Including you! Stop talking about my husband when yours is worse!"

Terri mashed the brake at the stoplight, which jolted Lisa forward. "I don't want you to make the same mistakes that I did. If you see a problem, get out of it before it's too late."

"I can't help it if you married the wrong man, but Doug is the right man for me. Just because you made a mistake doesn't mean that Doug and I won't work out."

"Look, if he starts coming in late with no explanation, don't say I didn't warn you."

"Wait, what? Is Ricky doing that to you?"

"It's nothing."

"Terri—"

"Forget I said anything, Lisa. I shouldn't have said anything." Terri wiped a wet trail from her tears off her cheek. "Forget it, okay?" She sniffed, pasted a fake smile on her face instead. "It's your wedding day! Forget I said anything."

Lisa stared at her sister, but some of her excitement was gone, and the rolling of her stomach wasn't all from the baby or all from her sister's marriage troubles alone.

Chapter 3

One Black Tux.

One happy groom.

One wedding ready to begin.

Doug stared into the mirror adjusting the sleeves on his shirt, thinking about the commitment he was about to make to the woman who captured his heart. He was getting married and their life was about to begin.

"You look great, Doug." Harold said.

The groomsman was running a comb through his unruly hair in the mirror above the bar.

Greg, Doug's best man, teased Doug, "Last chance to change your mind. I got the car out back. We can run out before she gets here."

Doug laughed. "No way! You and I both know I was doomed the day I met her. If I ran out now, I'd just find her again. Remember Miami? Went on a trip and there she was. Fate. Don't mess with fate."

Everyone laughed.

"You're right. I should've never said that. You were meant to be with Lisa no matter where you are or what you're doing." Greg smiled and Doug turned from the mirror, letting the other man straighten his already straight bowtie.

Todd knocked at the door and entered with his son Rhett. Doug nodded to his brother with a smile before looking down at his watch.

Almost time to get married.

"I still can't believe you're saying: 'I do.' Who am I going to chase women with now?"

Doug shook his head and laughed at Greg. "It's still your fault. You started it."

Greg grinned with Doug. "Me and my big mouth. Harold, why didn't you stop me?"

Harold laughed as well. "When have I ever been able to stop you from doing something stupid, Greg? Everyone knows Doug can't say no to a dare. 'Get the sistah's number,' you said. 'Bet you can't.'"

"And he couldn't…"

Harold rolled his eyes.

Doug smiled broader. "Fate, I was destined to be with her."

"Of course you were bruh." Greg shoulder bumped Doug.

Mona walked into the room and Doug moved to hug her, surprised at how relieved he was to see her there, knowing she was standing with him.

"I knew you would find the right woman. I just had to be patient until you did." Mona's dusty blue eye shadow enhanced the glow of pride in her eyes.

"Thanks, Aunt Mona." He gave her another hug. "I'm ready to get this started."

Todd joined duo, family together, always. "She's a good woman, Doug. You are fortunate to have found Lisa. May the both of you always find happiness with each other."

***

Lisa's conversation with Terri weighed on her thoughts while she dressed for the wedding.

What if Terri was right and the control moved to abuse?

It would be difficult to get rid of an abusive, well-connected man especially after she had his child.

Our marriage won't turn out that way. We love each other. It will work out.

Turning up the corners of her lip, she looked at her reflection. She was glad she chose the princess style dress that covered her pregnancy really well. The early morning trip to the hairdresser the day before was well worth the hours it took for her hair to look healthy and shine under her shoulder length veil.

Lisa finished applying the mulberry lipstick to her full lips, passing it to Terri put it away in her makeup bag.

"You look lovely," Ann said, as a few tears rolling down her cheek.

Lisa hugged her mother, "Thank you."

She released her mother to accept the bouquet of pink and white flowers that Terri passed to her.

Ann adjusted Lisa's veil, "You picked a good time for this wedding. Two weeks later and I don't think you would have fit into that dress."

"Mom," Lisa sighed. "The Justice of the Peace would have been just fine. Between you and Doug, this *small* wedding turned into a large one."

"You only do this once, so you may as well celebrate in style. Anyway, all of your soccer players wouldn't have been able to fit in the judge's chamber at the courthouse." Ann said as she placed the necklace around Lisa's throat. "Something old. And something borrowed."

Lisa positioned the locket around her neck to the center of her gown and smiled. "Aunt Nina's locket. It's beautiful."

"I want it back after the ceremony."

Lisa laughed. "All right, Mom." She smiled at she held onto the old gold piece of jewelry. "You're right. I'm glad all my players are here. They're my family too and it wouldn't be right without them." She shook her head and grinned at her mom, sister, and bridesmaids that were gathered around her. "I still can't believe how fast this has happened."

"I'll say."

Everyone laughed.

Terri approached Lisa. "I'm sorry about what I said earlier. I only wish you happiness. I love you, baby sis."

"I know, big sis." Her eyes watered and she handed her bouquet to her mom, laughing when Maya handed her a tissue to dab at her eyes. "No more sad stuff! Don't make me cry and ruin my makeup!"

Corey hugged her, and Terri hiccupped a laugh against Lisa's shoulder. "Don't you dare get eyeliner on my wedding dress. Sister or not, I'll kill you!"

Everyone laughed.

"You look beautiful, cuz," Stacy said. "I'm so happy for you."

Lisa took her younger cousin's hand, completing the circle of all the women in her wedding family, drawing them close to her. "Ok Mom, any last-minute words of advice?" She asked.

"Too late now. I'm just waiting for my grandchild,"

Lisa laughed at her mother.

Terri turned to the bridesmaids and said, "Well Stacy, Corey and Maya, it looks like you're the single ones in the group."

"Do you married, and soon to be married, women have words of advice for us single ladies?" Stacy asked.

Lisa grinned, "How about: don't live in a house with a single, rich, white guy. You might get pregnant."

The room burst into peals of laughter right before a knock sounded at the door.

Dave entered and stopped.

Lisa met her father's gaze and smiled at the love in his eyes.

He cleared his throat and she looked up as Maya dabbed at her eyes again and her mother gave her a final pat on the arm.

"Lisa, are you ready?"

"Yes."

Chapter 4

"It's time."

Jonah's voice and knock on the door interrupted Doug's nervousness. He straightened his black tie for the third time in the last ten minutes.

"You got this." Greg slapped his shoulder and grinned in the mirror with him. "Better you than me."

Doug nodded and took one last look before walking to the door. Jonah beckoned him with a wave of his hand. "Follow me please."

Followed by his groomsmen, he walked toward the increasing sound of music in Oxford Hall. As directed, he waited by the entranceway for their cue to come in.

"How long is this gonna be?" Rhett asked his dad. He fidgeted with his tie and tried to loosen it.

"Shhh." Todd said and yanked his arm. "Behave and leave the tie alone"

Doug chuckled to himself and wondered if Rhett would be able to stand still long enough for the ceremony. It was his cue to enter and the groomsmen followed.

Doug walked down the aisle. He saw many familiar and unfamiliar faces. He smiled while photographers and guests flashed pictures of him waiting at the improvised altar for his bride.

He faced everyone.

He was ready.

It was time and she was the one.

Greg leaned close to him. "There's still time to get out of here."

The bridesmaids walked down the aisle in their light rose gowns.

The ushers rolled the rice paper to the front of the aisle.

He watched the flower girl in her beautiful white gown gently dropping the rose petals and smiling brightly for the cameras.

Doug inhaled and took a deep breath. "No there isn't."

Lisa was always a stunning beauty.

Today she was beyond incredible. Her father guided her down the aisle, beaming with pride.

Lisa smiled beautifully, taking slow, deliberate steps towards him.

Doug almost met her halfway but knew he had to remain in place until she got closer.

It seemed like forever.

It took no time at all.

He took four steps to take her hand from her father, so enamored with her that he didn't realize the ceremony was waiting for him to proceed until the pastor cleared his throat.

Lisa gave him a slight squeeze of the hand, laughing with love at him. His cheeks heated, but he managed to turn back to the altar and Pastor Morris waiting for him to proceed.

He was ready to take his vows.

"Are you ready?" Doug whispered in Lisa's ear as he brought her close with his cheek resting against hers.

"I am." She said and smiled back at him.

"We are gathered here today…" started Reverend Morris.

Unbelievable.

I'm getting married.

I love you.

Greg tapped Doug's shoulder to hand him the ring.

He shook his head to clear his thoughts, managed to take the ring and slip it onto Lisa's finger without dropping it.

His grandmother's ring. Old and new. Family. Connection. Whole.

"Do you take this woman to be your wife?"

"I do."

"And do you Lisa Louise Dunbar; take Douglas Arthur Bader to be your wedded husband?"

Doug's heart was beating fast. He couldn't look away from Lisa's eyes.

She blinked and it was like looking into her soul, like falling into her beauty, warmth and love. A moment of time so perfect he would remember it, cherish it, for the rest of his life.

She looked to her side and he managed to pull himself to the present.

The cold platinum ring was a shock to his senses, a weight and an anchor to hold on to.

He looked down on it, the ring he would be wearing for a lifetime.

"I do." She said as she continued to stare into Doug's eyes.

"By the power vested in me, by the state of Georgia, I now pronounce you husband and wife. You may kiss your bride."

Doug lifted Lisa's veil.

Seconds turned to minutes. Minutes to hours. A lifetime in the soft press of his lips to hers. Not nearly long enough.

Their guests clapped and cheered.

Doug pulled slowly away and smiled, for the very first time, at his wife.

Chapter 5

"I love you." Lisa said as she pulled Doug close and brushed her nose against his. "This day is perfect."

Doug grinned back, "It is."

"One more photo?"

Doug wrapped his arm around Lisa's waist and she placed her hand in the center of his tuxedo and smiled for the picture.

"Are you hungry?" Doug asked.

"I am. I'll meet you in Dogwood Hall in ten minutes."

"I know," he grinned. "You have to go—"

"Yes," she nodded. "I'll see you shortly." Lisa motioned for Terri to come with her, leaving the interminable photographer behind to finally take a break, needing a moment to collect herself.

She was Mrs. Douglas Bader.

Terri took her arm and Lisa smiled at her sister. "I wondered how long you were going to hold out before needing to go."

Lisa laughed at her sister's comment, shaking her head, though it was true.

"I'll help you with your dress."

They stepped into the handicap stall and Terri helped Lisa step out of her gown.

She tripped over the fabric and almost fell over.

"Watch out. You almost ripped it. It's a good thing you wore slippers instead of heels"

"I got this." Lisa said as she balanced herself. "I'll be out in a minute."

Mrs. Douglas Arthur Bader.

I'm Mrs. Douglas Arthur Bader.

The pregnant Mrs. Douglas Arthur Bader.

"Lisa, do you need me to help you in there?" Terri said.

"I'm fine. I just need a minute to put all of this back on."

"Okay. Your guests are waiting."

Lisa came out of the stall and Terri assisted her with slipping her gown back on.

"You look so beautiful Lisa!" She hugged her sister again.

"Thank you. I still can't believe I just got married." Terri handed Lisa her bouquet. She took a whiff of the flowers. "Ooh, they smell so wonderful."

"We've got to go. Family and friends are waiting to take pictures. I'm so happy for you."

***

Lisa found Doug in Oxford Hall talking with Mark Steward, a partner at Whitman Stacks. She slipped her hand into his and smiled when Doug drew her into his side.

"We were just talking about all the teenagers here. I didn't know you coached girls' soccer."

She smiled at the older man. "Yes sir, girls' soccer is a passion of mine. I played for several years amateur and professionally. There are several coaches here as well."

The smell of the rosemary garlic chicken drifted through the air increasing her hunger pains and the growling of her stomach confirmed that it was time to eat. She hoped that Mark didn't hear it.

Doug noticed right away and glanced over at her.

She pretended as if nothing happened.

"I recognized a few people. I'm friends with Arnold who's a board member of your soccer club."

Lisa smiled, "Yes, I know him. His wife organized the fundraiser we had last year."

"Oh. I remember, Doug attended in my place, I had a conflict." Lisa looked up and smiled at Doug. "I remember that speech. It was the first time I saw you with your glasses."

Doug returned the smile. "I remember it too." He squeezed her hand securely intertwining his fingers in hers.

Mark extended his hand. "Congratulations to you both."

"Thank you," they both responded. Mark walked away leaving the pair alone.

Doug reached in his coat pocket, pulled out a granola bar and handed it to her. "For you. Dinner won't be served for a few more minutes and I don't want you to faint."

She grinned; grateful that Doug's paranoia about her pregnancy saved the day. "Oh, thank you, I'm starved." She tore off the wrapper and munched down the snack quickly.

He brushed the crumbs from her lips and gave her a quick kiss. "We have a few more guests to attend to."

Chapter 6

"Dear Lord, we gather in this place in a spirit of celebration and gratitude. Thank you for the blessing of bringing Doug and Lisa together in marriage today. We ask you to bless their union, their family, and all their relationships. Please bless this food we are about to receive, and let this reception be an honor to you. In Jesus' name. Amen."

Pastor Morris placed his hands on both Doug and Lisa's shoulders. He nodded to Greg, who stood up from the table with his glass in hand.

"The best man, Mr. Greg Speaks will now make the toast to the bride and groom."

Pastor Morris passed the microphone over.

Glasses clinked as guests used the transition moment to clink their glasses, hollering for a kiss from the bride and groom.

Doug obligated to cheers from the guests.

Greg tapped his shoulder. "C'mon now. This is going to be hard enough."

Doug turned around with a teasing grin, "You're next and you know it,"

"I've got to get this over with," laughed Greg. Raising his glass from the table, he smiled back at the guests. "Doug and I go back many years. We've been best friends since high school. Although we went to different universities, we've always kept in touch. We chased many women together…" He turned his body and lowered his eyes as he looked at Lisa, "Sorry, Lisa."

Lisa responded with a laugh and she squeezed Doug's hand.

"Doug and I both were confirmed bachelors."

Doug grinned.

"That day ended when we were in a restaurant and I bet Doug that he couldn't get Lisa's number." Greg paused, took in a deep breath and exhaled slowly. "Well, I won that bet, but decided not to charge him for dinner."

Lisa and Doug both chuckled. She leaned over and kissed him on the cheek.

"Doug and I both knew that his life was changed forever that night. He and Lisa kept meeting over and over again. Doug decided to make his move, and the rest, we just saw, is history."

Greg glanced down at his newly married friend with a half joking grin. "Now I'm chasing women by myself and Doug will not let me live that down."

Greg fumbled with the microphone in his hand and turned back to face the guests. "Lisa has taken Doug off the market leaving all the single women for me. My phone number is…" Laughter echoed throughout Dogwood Hall.

Greg chuckled and smiled. "But the women are not the only ones disappointed. Doug has explicitly informed every male within one hundred miles of Lisa that she is taken. Secured. Off-limits. His…caveman style, if necessary." Doug tilted back in his chair and roared with laughter.

Greg raised his glass higher along with the guests. He turned to the couple and leaned forward from the waist for a mid-bow. "My congratulations to the both of you and may you have a long and happy marriage."

***

Lisa looked down at her plate and realized that she didn't have the full serving of extra potatoes that she requested. She motioned for the server to come by.

"Can I have an extra potato serving? It was supposed to be with the course."

"Wait, Lisa, I cancelled that."

She turned her gaze to her husband. "What? Do you realize how hungry I am?" She tried to keep her tone pleasant, but between her hunger pains and the stress of the day, she wasn't sure she was succeeding. "Are you trying to starve this baby?"

Doug's cheeks flushed as he realized she was right. This was a long day and she needed more nutrients than normal. Extra potatoes couldn't hurt.

He hesitated. "I'll let you have mine. I'm looking out for you and our baby." Doug moved his serving over to Lisa's plate.

Terri snickered at Lisa's side.

She snapped at her sister, "Not a word from you."

Terri threw her hands up but didn't say anything.

***

"It's time to cut the cake."

Good! I can't wait to taste this."

A happy Doug pulled Lisa to the table with the desserts on it. He handed her the knife with *Mr. and Mrs. Douglas Arthur Bader* etched along the side of the blade. "I trust you with this."

Lisa smiled back and raised her eyebrows, "You do?"

"I do." He said still smiling. She selected a layer to slice; Doug covered his hand over hers and guided her to press down on the first incision. She pulled her hand to select a large piece of cake and He resisted. She struggled more to make the bigger slice and he gave way.

"I'll feed it to you." He took the fork and gave her a small bite."

"You've got to do better than that, Mr. Bader."

"That's enough sugar for the baby."

"That's the only sugar I've had all day, it's *my* wedding cake!"

Doug didn't budge.

"Fine." Lisa restrained her temper and smiled coolly at her new husband. "It's my turn to feed you."

Lisa took the plate and the fork. She swiped a large bite for herself before lifting the rest of the same piece of cake and offered it to him.

"Open up."

As he opened his mouth, she smashed the cake into his face with the remaining chocolate swirl mix covering his nose, chin and portions of his tuxedo.

Doug took a napkin and laughed. "I deserved that one, huh?"

Lisa laughed. "You sure did." She leaned forward and kissed the icing and crumbs off his face. "But I'm stuck with you anyways. Love you, sweetie."

Chapter 7

The roads were clear and the ride was smooth around I-285 to the Hilton hotel after the reception. Doug reserved the executive suite as a surprise to Lisa before their honeymoon. He glanced over at his sleeping bride, happy with the woman he chose to be with for a lifetime.

She was perfect.

Just enough spitfire to keep him interested and more than enough femininity to hold his attention on all levels. Her silky smooth brown skin was gentle to touch and her soft body cushioned his firm muscles. He loved being with her and sharing their time on physical and emotional levels.

He knew that he harbored secrets. Secrets that he wasn't ready to share. Maybe someday he would. He trusted her, but it wasn't about trusting her, it was about him being ready to share some of the dark days in his past.

She was giving him life and a new start to be happy.

He didn't want to darken that.

He listened to the light snores that exhaled through her mouth.

Exhausted. She had to be with the pregnancy and the full events of the day. His sleeping beauty needed rest for now.

Why did it take so long before she appeared? It didn't matter now. She is Mrs. Douglas Arthur Bader and she has my ring on her finger to prove it.

"Where are we?" Lisa said, rousing slightly in her seat next to him. "What time is it?'

"We're ten minutes from the hotel. Relax. You can go back to sleep until we get there. Anyways, you'll be up the rest of the night." He winked at her.

His tone perked her interest. "Do tell, Mr. Bader." She didn't feel much like sleeping anymore and grinned. "You won't be able to keep up with me."

"Promise?" Doug chuckled.

"Promise."

"Get the rest of your nap so you can make good on that promise."

***

"Well this is nice," exclaimed Lisa as they both entered the executive suite of the hotel. "Too bad we leave early in the morning. We could spend a few days here."

Doug dropped the overnight bag by the door and wrapped Lisa in his arms. "I knew you would like it. It's our first night together, married, and I want you to remember it."

"I will never forget it." She popped a few buttons on the lower section of his shirt."

He pulled her in tight.

She paused tilting her head back and looking in his eyes.

He smiled. "I still can't believe we're married."

"I can't believe it either. It's a good thing that it's on video. I might deny this in the morning."

He laughed. "Don't you dare." He grinned. "Greg offered to help me escape. I wouldn't have. I had to marry you. Somehow, I knew that no matter where I was, you would be there with me. But he did offer."

She snorted. "Where would you have escaped to? I think that I would have cleared my head and went to Noel's House of Jazz."

A smile swept across his face as he reached into his pants pocket, pulled out a light green piece of paper and handed it to her.

She read the notice.

Noel's House of Jazz Presents
Jazz Singer Addie Miles
One Night Only

"Ahhhh," Lisa shrieked and stepped back. "We were meant to be together. I can't believe this. Where did you get this?"

"Greg. He gave it to me while I was dressing for the wedding. It looks like either way; I was going to see you today."

"Ooh, I love you," She wrapped her arms around his waist and raised her chin for an incoming kiss.

"Not yet. We are having our own private toast. Come with me."

Taking her by the hand, he led her to the kitchen and opened the refrigerator. One chilled bottle of sparkling grape juice and the finest Godiva chocolate he could find.

She breathed, "Chocolate's not on my diet."

"It is today." He reached for a couple of glasses from the cabinet, poured the bubbly in a flute and passed it to her. She pursed her lips to take a sip.

"Not yet."

He opened the box and unwrapped a dark chocolate treat.

"Open up."

Obediently, she closed her eyes and savored the sugary morsel and the incoming kiss that soon followed.

"Mmmm."

He helped her raise her glass of sparkling grape juice. "Sip."

"Yes."

"Yes." Doug breathed as he reached behind her and loosened the back of her gown.

She delighted in his lips pressed against hers and unbuckled his pants.

"Oooh, here?" Lisa asked.

He licked the shell of her ear, nuzzled against her lobe. "Wherever you want," he answered, his deep, low Southern drawl made heat flare below her waist.

She slid his shirt slid down his well-toned arms.

Her wedding dress slipped to a puddle of white on the floor.

He slipped his fingers beneath the clasp of her bra, pulled the silken straps down her arms and bared her breasts to his gaze. He leaned forward, placed a warm kiss against the pulse at the side of her throat, nipped, and slid his lips down her collarbone, across the sloping curve of her breast.

His arms snaked around her waist and upper back. He held her steady when she leaned back, baring herself to him. His breath raised pebbles across her skin that he chased with his tongue. She moaned above him feeling a fire rush through her veins and she couldn't get to all natural fast enough.

With a firm grip under her thigh, Doug laid his bride on the pool of white satin and parted her legs so that he could taste the woman of his dreams.

She squealed.

She moaned.

She howled loud enough to let the galaxy know that the peak of her pleasure was reached.

He lifted his head and crawled to bring his face to hers. She took short quick breaths and puckered her lips.

"It's not over yet. Mrs. Bader." He covered her lips his muffling any verbal reaction she could possibly have.

Tracing the inside of her thigh, he plunged his fingers between her hips with a swift and deliberate motion. He increased his vibrating motion throughout her inner walls. His first claim to territory now labeled "Wife"

"Ooh" she panted. Beads of perspiration were soaking her warm yet chilled body.

Removing his fingers, he lifted his upper body and shifted his thighs inside of hers. The second claim to territory posted its mark firmly. Her tightened hips loosening enough to receive all of him.

"Uh, Uh, Uh." He huffed. *Mine. All mine.* His pace sped faster and faster.

Her lips parted but the air moving through them was reserved to chase paradise with her lover, her husband.

She dug her nails into his arms.

The small prick only spurred him faster, higher.

She wrapped her legs tight around his hips shifting herself with each thrust to keep up with his pace. Lisa reached her peak. "Aaah."

"Yes." His body tremored and the movement of his hips slowed down. He held himself over his bride and shook his head to relax his body.

She pulled him to lay beside her on the dress.

He nestled on top of the sequins, ignoring the pinch of the tiny embellishments on his skin.

"I love you."

Chapter 8

"Does this remind you of anything?" asked Doug as he held his Wall Street Journal in his lap. He fastened his seatbelt. A few passengers were in the aisles loading luggage in the upper racks.

"Absolutely," Lisa smiled as she took his hand. "But I've got the window seat this time." She turned her head to look out of the window of her business class seat.

"We haven't flown since the pregnancy." He raised their linked fingers to his lips. "I'm here for you."

She turned from the window and blushed at his actions, "I love that you're here for me." She adjusted the seatbelt over her belly. "We'll have a great time in Miami."

"This is such a short trip," he complained. "Only four days?"

"I know but we both agreed to take a longer trip later after the baby is born. Besides, you have a big case to prepare for. I want our honeymoon to be about us, not you dragging a suitcase full of work."

Doug raised his eyebrows and smiled broadly, "Did you pack the red bathing suit that you wore the last time we were here?"

Lisa struck him on the arm. "No silly," she patted her stomach, "I'm a little out of shape for that."

"I don't think so. You're hot with it on and off."

Lisa laughed with embarrassment. "Everyone on the plane doesn't need to know that."

***

The weather was perfect for February in Miami. The afternoon was in the high 70's and the sun was shining. The cool breeze swirled through the open windows of their rental car. The ride was thirty-minutes to South Beach Hotel.

They arrived for an early afternoon check in. Doug had heard about the hotel from a parent at the library. He'd researched the amenities and believed that it would be a romantic and exclusive get away for him and Lisa.

The reality was better than the pictures. The courtyard had several palm trees and he could see signs pointing to private beach access as they walked into the lobby.

"Welcome to the South Beach Hotel. My name is Susie. Are you checking in?"

"Yes. Mr. and Mrs. Douglas Bader."

"I see. I have your reservation here," Doug felt a little pale as Susie was talking. He kept looking at her strangely. Lisa was oblivious to his reaction.

Should I tell her?

She should know. Right?

Maybe she doesn't know.

"Sir, you reserved the Jr. King Suite. Is that correct?"

"Eh, yes." Doug managed to get through the reservation process and flashed his platinum American Express card to pay for the room. Once she handed him the access cards, he couldn't resist. "You shouldn't be working right now. You should be in bed. You're putting your baby in danger."

The hotel clerk paused in shock. Lisa whipped around and saw the deadpan gaze on Doug's face.

"You must be mistaken sir. I'm not pregnant."

Doug persisted, "If I were you, I would see a doctor right away. Your hands are swollen and your face is flush. You may be further along than you realize." Based on his observation, there was no mistake that woman was pregnant and he was the first person to tell her

Susie couldn't take her eyes off Doug. Another clerk was behind the counter and walked over to stand beside her. She stared at Doug with a curious puzzled look on her face still taking in his outburst.

Lisa tugged on his shirtsleeve, which broke him out of his trance.

He smiled at Lisa, leaning in to kiss her, hoping she would forget about this incident. "Never mind."

He grabbed the handle of the suitcase and walked away from the desk with Lisa following his lead to the elevator.

"What was that about?" Lisa asked.

"Not here," he said shaking his head. "Let's discuss it a little later."

The ride was silent in the elevator.

Doug gave her the key to enter the room while he brought in the bags. He dropped the bags once inside the door, locked it behind him, before walking to the window to gaze out at the ocean.

Lisa joined him and wrapped her arms around his waist. "Why did you tell her that?"

Doug turned from the window and looked in her eyes. "She's sick. I thought she knew that she was pregnant."

"But how did you know? What if you're wrong? What if she isn't pregnant?"

"I'm positive she is." He changed the subject. "Are you hungry?"

She let him. "Starved. I'm craving red meat."

"That's not good for you, Lisa."

Lisa frowned at him, "It's *our* honeymoon, Doug. We're supposed to eat steak and lobster. We're supposed to splurge on our honeymoon!"

"It's *your* pregnant honeymoon, sweetheart. And that means not as much splurging as you might otherwise have been allowed."

Been allowed?

She opened her mouth to tell him what he was *allowed,* but he smiled at her with his baby blues, and she bit her lip. Compromise. Trust. Love. Til death do them part. "What if we split a steak? I've got to have some red meat."

"Perfect."

She watched the tension ease from his shoulders.

"You can have three bites." He pulled her hands into his chest and placed them over his heart.

"That doesn't sound like half…"

He laughed and pressed his forehead to hers. "Think about the baby, Lisa."

"They had better be three big bites."

***

Tika's Steak House wasn't far from the hotel, so Lisa suggested that they walk. They got to the restaurant early. Since reservations weren't required, they were seated right away.

"Let's go shopping tomorrow for maternity clothes. I've been so busy preparing for the wedding that I haven't thought about what I'll need as the baby gets bigger."

"We'll go early and have lunch in town." Doug slid his hand under the table to grab hers.

She winked at him.

He met her gaze for a moment before looking past her towards the ocean. She noticed his eyes glazed over and his cheek muscles relaxed.

"I'm beginning to learn your habits. I feel like I've been married to you forever. What's on your mind?"

He shook his head, shrugged and chuckled. "What do you think about me starting my own practice?"

Lisa grinned. *It's about time you got away from that firm. The Lily White Southern Boy's Club.* "I think it's a great idea. You'll never make partner in that firm being married to me."

"Lisa!"

"It's true and you know it."

Doug wanted to defend his partners, but she was right. He didn't want to admit it, but she was; it was just their world.

"When?" Lisa asked.

"After the baby is born. I'll be ready to handle medical malpractice suits by then."

"Wow! What made you decide to go into medical malpractice? I know that you have the medical background but I understood that you wanted to stay away from the medical field."

He sipped his water before speaking, "I think it's time. I've stayed out of medicine for personal reasons but it's time for me to go back to it. I loved medicine before the accident. I'm beginning to miss practicing medicine again."

Another flutter from the baby caused Lisa to lean back in her chair to allow the stretch she felt she needed. "I think you're excited about the pregnancy. You should see yourself when you're in the office with me on the doctor's visits. It's as if you want to take over and perform the exam. I know my doctor is getting annoyed."

He laughed, "I know he is. Competing schools of thoughts." He cut into his steak and gave her a few pieces to add to her grilled chicken.

She forked the first bite before he'd finished putting it on her plate. "Why did you go into law?"

"I went into law because I missed the challenges and the discipline of the classroom. Practicing divorce law is unique in that you meet many people who can't resolve their differences. The heated debates between the couples have taught me a lot. Usually the marriage is over when they come to me.

"I need you to turn your head." Lisa said.

"Why?"

"Because I'm taking more steak and I don't want to have to stab you with my fork to get it."

"Lisa, red meat isn't good for the baby. Only in small portions. I forbid—"

She narrowed her eyebrows and frowned. "Forbid!" exclaimed Lisa.

Doug raised his hand to avoid a confrontation. "I'm going to the restroom. We'll continue the discussion when I get back." His eyes stared directly in hers. He nodded and threw his napkin on the table before rising, a silent signal that he wasn't going to watch her eat more steak than she should.

Lisa waited until he was out of site and grabbed as much as she desired.

She couldn't believe that they were about to argue again regarding the amount of food she should have while pregnant. She considered not grabbing any steak, but she wasn't going to let him win.

At least not tonight.

***

Doug looked at the remaining steak on his plate when he got back to the table.

They were on their honeymoon. He should relax but the baby was just too important not to help her realize that he was doing what was best for her and the child.

He wanted her to listen to him and not give him so much resistance.

It was her independence that attracted him to her.

Lisa smiled as he glanced at the missing steak on his plate. She digested *her* half of the spicy steak with a smile. She wouldn't talk about it, wouldn't bring it back up, and let it go, for the sake of their honeymoon.

They'd been talking about his divorce cases.

She could deal with that. "It's a good thing we agreed to the terms in the pre-nup. Why did it take you so long to bring it up? We almost waited too late to have one."

He looked over at his new bride. She looked stunning. Maybe a little red meat wouldn't hurt her. After all, they were on their honeymoon and he wanted to have a good time with his wife. He wanted to enjoy their honeymoon with minimal disagreements. "Everything moved so fast. I thought we'd have a long engagement. I didn't expect you to get pregnant so soon. Once we found out, a pre-nup almost didn't make sense. Our better option was to write a will for custody of the baby in case anything happened to us, and have a written power of attorney. I'm glad the paperwork is signed." The waitress brought the signed copy of the credit card bill for dinner.

She wiped her mouth and put the napkin in the middle of her plate. "Do you want to take a walk around the hotel this evening?" she asked.

He flashed a smile. "Sure."

When they arrived back to the hotel, Doug noticed a male hotel clerk motioning him to come to the desk. Doug shrugged it off and answered the summons.

"Just after you left, Susie fainted. We had an ambulance rush her to the hospital. Her family called a few minutes ago, she lost the baby. How did you know when she didn't?"

Doug answered, "Medical training and a gift. I'm sorry to hear about Susie. I hope she gets better soon."

Chapter 9

Knock, Knock, Knock

"Housekeeping."

"Go away," he growled, rolling over towards his sleeping bride. "Come later."

The knocking stopped and Doug caressed her arm gently and listened to the soft snoring sound she was making. He was becoming accustomed to her rhythmic pattern. It meant she was here next to him.

He placed his fingers on her firm abdomen. Would the baby look like him or Lisa?

The baby would be a mix of the two of them. The best of both. Their legacy together.

The room had a crisp chill and his love shivered beneath the light covers. He held her closer to warm her cooled body.

She nestled next him while still asleep.

"What time is it?" murmured Lisa. She placed her hand over his, intertwining their fingers in such a way that the metal on the new wedding rings were touching to symbolize the infinity of their union.

"After nine. I know you're hungry."

"How can you tell?"

"I heard your stomach growling and we're a little off schedule." He lowered his hand below her abdomen and traced the inside of her thighs.

She placed her hand over his and guided him to caress her gently. "We'll never eat if we start this," she cooed.

"I can think of one thing I'd like for breakfast." Doug lowered the covers and placed his lips between her thighs, tasting every inch between her knees and torso.

She parted her legs wider to receive every kiss and brushed her fingers through his locks.

He increased his taste test to a full meal of his bride.

"Oooh," she moaned and tightened her grip on his curly locks.

She orgasmed with a cry, clutching him to her, head thrown back in the pillows, gasping for air that came in small short breaths.

Her smiling groom climbed beside her. "I bet you're really hungry now."

"I am." She cooed and threw her head back on the pillows. "Let's get up for breakfast soon."

***

"What's this?" Lisa asked after stepping out of the shower with only a towel and a smile.

"A little something I picked up for you as a wedding gift." He placed a small red box with a green bow in her hand.

"It's not Christmas or my birthday," she popped the lid off the box and screamed. "Diamond earrings! How did you know I wanted a pair?"

"A lucky guess."

Lisa put them on and hugged him. "I'm a lucky bride."

"You are."

"You're so arrogant."

"And you love it."

"I do." Lisa pressed her lips against his for a short kiss. "I'm starved."

"Finish dressing and we'll go shopping."

She closed the bathroom door.

His cell phone rang.

He didn't recognize the number, but answered anyways. "It's Bader."

"It's Veronica. We met last year at the summer picnic for troubled youth. I just found your number. How are you?"

"Great. I'm on my honeymoon." Doug half whispered and hoped Lisa didn't hear him. He'd thought all his calls stopped when he got engaged, but his number was out there and lots of women had it.

"Oh, I didn't mean to intrude. You have a great time, bye."

"Bye." Doug looked over at the bathroom door and hoped that Lisa didn't hear the conversation.

Moments later, the door opened.

She walked over to him and gave him a hug. "Was that Mona calling?"

"Nah," he smirked, "Wrong number."

"It's your turn to get dressed. I'm calling my mom while you're in the shower."

"I'll be out shortly." He brushed his lips against her cheek and headed to the shower. The hot steam opened his pores and the thoughts came rushing in.

Your past is going to catch up with you.

How long before someone else calls.

It'd been almost six months since he had women calling.

You almost got caught doing something that you didn't do. So why lie about it?

She wouldn't understand. That's why.

I ended that life and I'm in love with Lisa.

***

After lunch, Doug and Lisa came back to the hotel to access the private beach entrance and take a walk. Holding hands and feeling the sand under their feet, they walked toward the water to dip their toes in the ocean.

"This is cold," Lisa shivered.

Doug wrapped his arms around her and brought her in close. "I'll keep you warm."

Lisa fingered his shirt, "I bet you will."

"Did you enjoy lunch?" he asked as he walked her away from the ocean and towards the sand.

"That seafood salad was amazing. How was your Chilean sea bass?"

"Great. Do you want to rest and go out later?" He didn't want Lisa to overdo and was ready for more alone time together on their honeymoon.

"No, I'm fine." She said and dismissed his worry about her condition. "We still haven't gone shopping yet and my clothes are getting too small."

"Sure. We'll go."

The wind picked up a little and blew threw his curls.

Lisa shivered again. "I should have brought a sweater."

"There's one in the suitcase. Let's go to the room and get it before we head downtown."

***

"Oh, look." Lisa said as they were on their way to the maternity store, "that lady has triplets."

Doug turned in the direction that Lisa was pointing. Three toddler children with matching green soccer shirts were playing on the indoor playground. Lisa pulled Doug to walk over and get a closer look.

"We'll be doing that really soon. Do you want to sit and watch for a minute? There's a coffee shop nearby."

Lisa spotted an empty table. "There, I can watch them play for a while."

Doug followed her lead and they grabbed an empty table. "I'm getting hot chocolate. Do you want some?"

"I am your hot chocolate."

Doug snickered. "Yes, you are. I'll be right back." He walked away to order from the nearby coffee shop.

The mother of the toddlers plucked them from the playground one by one and strapped them in the stroller. She wheeled them close to Lisa.

"They're beautiful," she said. "How do you get them to behave at that age?"

"Luck," the woman answered exhaustedly. "Today was a better day than others. I usually have my mom with me, but she's at my sister's house. I was brave enough to come out on my own."

"I see you're a soccer fan."

The woman smiled, "I am. My husband and I both played. I'm sorry to be rude. I'm Dotty." She extended her hand.

"Lisa."

Dotty's eyebrows narrowed with a curious expression on her face.

Lisa turned to see what she was looking at and nearly bashed her face against Doug's as he leaned in close to her. She shook her head, laughing as she patted his cheek and pulled away. "This is my husband, Doug."

Dotty smiled. "Nice to meet you."

A bottle went flying across the mall floor.

"That's my cue. I have to get them to sleep or I'll never get any myself. Take care." Dotty darted to retrieve the bottle and Lisa watched her leave.

She picked up her hot chocolate and took a sip.

"I'm glad we only have one coming," Doug laughed. "You would kill me if we had triplets."

Lisa waved him away. "Nah, that's why they have live-in nannies."

"You mean the young, hot Swedish ones?" he asked.

"No. Of course not. The military Austrian type nannies with muscles bigger than yours. I'm envisioning Arnold Schwarzenegger."

"Ow. That hurt," he laughed and took the lid off his hot chocolate for a sip. The white creamy foam lined his upper lip and he wiped it away.

"You started it," she chuckled. She took the stirrer and flicked some hot chocolate at him.

"You just wait until we get back to the hotel. I'm going to make you pay for that."

"Promise."

"Promise."

Chapter 10

"No soccer this weekend," breathed Lisa. She nestled herself beside Doug in their king size bed at Atlanta home.

They were married a week and all was well.

Her sandy blonde Adonis was next to her, peeking through his eyes and waking up for the day.

"No soccer for you, but story telling for me. I should get to the library around ten." He covered his mouth and yawned. "I'm going to the treadmill. I haven't been on it for a week."

"I'm getting up. I'm hungry. How about biscuits and sausage gravy?"

"No!" Doug said emphatically. "Not for you either. That's too heavy."

"I'm pregnant and hungry. Are we having this argument again?"

"One biscuit for you." He sat back on the bed, leaned over and traced his tongue behind her ear to ease the tension he felt building between them.

She softened at his touch.

"We're in agreement. You're having one too. If you don't eat it, I'll finish it for you."

"Oh. Twenty extra minutes on the treadmill." He got up and sassed at Lisa. "My manly figure can't take the calories."

"Just get on the treadmill," she ordered. "I'm getting out of bed in thirty minutes."

Forty minutes later, Doug was working his pacer on the treadmill. Permeating the air was the smell of eggs and sausage. His mom cooked that for breakfast on the weekends when they didn't have to rush to school.

She stayed home and worked part-time as a bookkeeper at the family business Bader Construction until Doug was a teenager. When the business got bigger, they hired a full-time bookkeeper. His mom stayed home and worked on her hobbies.

She'd encouraged him to be the avid reader that he is today. He took several advanced science classes, which allowed him to graduate early from high school. He loved science because it helped him understand his world around him.

"Are you coming to have breakfast?" Lisa shouted to him.

"In a few," he replied. He turned off the machine and bounded up the stairs to the shower.

***

When Doug came into the kitchen, the table was clean except for a plate covered in plastic wrap with leftover breakfast. The coffee was on the burner warming and Lisa was reading a book at the end of the kitchen table.

"Thanks for saving some for me." He grabbed an orange from the counter and brought it to the table.

"You're welcome." She smiled.

"Are you sure you don't want to come with me today to the library?" Doug took the plate of biscuits, sausage and eggs and placed it in the microwave to heat up.

"No, not today. I want to rest up. Have fun."

"Okay." Doug grabbed his food from the microwave and sat next to Lisa. There was a small stack of books on the table. "What's this?"

"I got you a few children's books for black history month. Even though I'm not going, I thought your little readers might enjoy these stories."

Black History Month?

"Oh, yea, I remember doing that in school. George Washington Carver and the peanut thing. I did a book report in eighth grade on him. The library does something for that every year."

"Black history month is more than Martin Luther King and Frederick Douglas. We have many African Americans that contributed to society. Their contribution to history was erased because of their color. That's why we celebrate it for the entire month."

Doug picked up the books and looked at the authors. Virginia Hamilton. Angela Johnson. Mildred Taylor. He didn't know that there were African American authors that wrote children's books. He wasn't going to divulge that to Lisa.

He leafed through the pages of one of the books. The main characters were all African American. It took him a moment to reflect on his sobering reality that he would be a father to a daughter or son that would be considered black. His children would want to read stories about children who looked like them.

"Mr. Bader, what are you thinking about?"

He shook his head and turned his gaze back to his Lisa. "You, my lovely wife," he smiled and continued to eat his breakfast. "I'll take these with me. I'm sure the kids will enjoy them."

Chapter 11

"What to do today?" Lisa asked herself after Doug walked out the door. She dressed earlier while Doug was on the treadmill and was a little too restless to go back to sleep. Her real purpose for staying home was to have some private time. She loved her husband, but sometimes he crowded her personal space.

"I know who to call." Lisa rushed to the living room to find the phone exactly where she'd left it last night. Her best friend was on speed dial.

"It's Corey."

"What's going on? Are you free today?"

"Well, if it isn't the honeymooner. I thought you'd be still in the bed with your husband. You've got time for me now?"

Lisa laughed. "Of course I do. Let's shop and do lunch."

"I'm in," Corey responded with excitement, "and I'll come pick you up."

"When?"

"I'll be there in thirty minutes."

"Great. Doug's gone for a while and I need a break. I've got to eat some red meat and Doug isn't cooperating."

Corey laughed, "I'll take you to get a hamburger at the Hamburger Stop. There's plenty of red meat there."

Twenty minutes later Corey arrived and they were on their way to the mall.

***

"And that wraps up this story. Thank you, everyone, for coming."

Doug put away the books he'd brought in a duffel bag. He stood up to stretch and get ready to leave. An unfamiliar mother approached him.

"Hi, I'm Kris. Jennifer is my daughter."

"Doug," he extended his hand to shake hers.

"I've got a question."

"Sure, go right ahead."

"Why did you pick the black peoples' book with kids in it?"

Doug was puzzled by her question and wasn't sure how to respond. "It's black history month."

"Yes, but that's for school kids. My kid is a toddler and doesn't need to know about that yet." Kris motioned for her daughter to stay put in a chair.

"Know about what?" Doug asked.

"Black people."

"I still don't understand your concern."

"You know. Gang bangers, drug dealers, hookers and welfare mothers. I don't want my daughter exposed to that."

"My wife is African American and she is none of those things." Doug's icy blue eyes narrowed and his jaw tightened.

This woman knew so little about African Americans that she had them in four categories.

Maybe Lisa was right.

He'd been oblivious to the racist thoughts of others and now that he was married to Lisa and having children with her, he had to be more aware of these things.

Kris slung her yellow purse over her arm. "Well I think you should pick something else to read to toddlers."

The atmosphere is the library was getting warm and so was his temper. "Ma'am. I have better things to do with my time than to argue my reading selections with you. If you will excuse me." Doug walked away.

***

Slamming the door when he walked through his North Atlanta home, Doug threw his keys on the kitchen table. They skidded past the bouquet of red roses centered on the table and landed on a chair.

Racism was alive and well, and young parents were teaching it their children.

"Lisa!" he shouted.

No response.

"Lisa!" He shouted angrily and walked through the living room to see if she was there.

He went to the landing of the stairs and called out again. "Lisa!"

Maybe she's asleep?

Bounding up the stairs, he arrived at their bedroom. The bed was made and the room was empty.

Running fast down the stairs to the basement, he looked for her.

No Lisa.

Back up the stairs and through the kitchen door to the garage, her car was in its usual spot.

"She said she wanted to rest."

He reached in his pocket and checked his phone.

No missed calls.

Panicked, he dialed her number.

"I'm unable to take your call—"

Doug hung up the phone and began searching the house again for her. He came back to the kitchen and looked to see if there was a note on the table.

Nothing.

Where the hell is she?

Who should he call first?

He went into the office and searched for Lisa's soccer papers. He found a list of phone numbers of kids and their parents.

"Too many numbers."

Running his fingers through the hair on the back of his head, he scanned his brain rapidly for the first person he should call.

Her parents.

What if she's not there?

Maybe she's at the hospital.

He dialed her number again and it went back to voicemail.

"Oh Lisa, if you're okay, you're going to pay for this."

Pacing the floor, Doug scratched through his hair still brainstorming.

Did I miss something this morning?

Maybe she went for a walk.

He walked outside, looked up and down the street and still no Lisa.

"I'm calling again." He said.

Finally, an answer.

"Hi, Doug."

Doug shouted through the phone. "Where are you? I've been calling for thirty minutes. You didn't say that you were going out."

"I'm out with Corey and I'll be home in a little while."

"Next time let me know, leave a note, something. I can't go through this."

"Go through what? I just went out for a little while." She huffed.

"Not knowing where you are. You can't just disappear. I looked all over for you. Don't ever—"
Click

"Damn!" he threw the phone down and papers flew to the floor.

***

Lisa sat back stunned from her conversation with Doug. She couldn't believe how panicked and angry he was that she was only out for a little while. She didn't think that she had to report all her time to him and wasn't sure how this inevitable argument was going to turn out.

"Is everything okay?" Corey asked. "Was it a good idea for us to get out this afternoon?"

"I guess Doug was worried that I wasn't home. He says I should have left a note."

Corey took a French fry and dipped it into her ketchup. "Well, you do have to report in when you're married. It's not just you. You are also pregnant." She hesitated before adding, "But he seems really over protective and demanding to me."

"Not you too. I argued with Terri over it. I know Doug has some control issues but nothing I can't handle." Lisa picked the pickles off her sandwich because she couldn't decide if she wanted them on her burger or not. She dipped them in the mustard and discovered a new treat.

"He's more controlling than most men that I know. I couldn't believe it when he showed up to the bridal shower and ordered food for you. That was insane."

Lisa crunched her pickles. "We're always arguing over my diet but I think he's just over protective of me and the baby. I'll be glad when this little one gets here. It's got to get better after that."

"It may get worse. He'll be controlling two diets. Just be careful, Lisa, and know where you stand."

***

Lisa arrived home and found Doug in the living room watching a documentary on the evolution of birds. She kissed him on the cheek and he reached for her hand. She sat down next to him.

"Sorry I didn't let you know I was out."

He glanced at her and responded in a restrained tone. "I was concerned when you didn't answer your phone. I thought we'd eat something and then go shopping at Ray's. I need a few ties."

"We can go in about an hour. I want to take a quick nap."

"Did you eat?" he asked relaxing the tension in his shoulders.

"Yes. Corey and I had lunch."

Doug shifted his weight on the couch and turned to face her. "What did you eat?"

Lisa immediately got defensive. "We're not having this conversation. I'm sick of this argument over food. I'm pregnant. Let me eat. My body knows what's best for our baby."

"Why won't you listen to me?" Doug rose from the couch. "I guess my degrees and papers are all hogwash and I don't know what the hell I'm talking about!"

Lisa stood and glared back at him. "I'm not your control toy. I'm sick of this argument. You want to tell me how to eat, when to exercise, how much time to sleep and I don't get any private time away from you without you demanding where I am. This is supposed to be a marriage, not a dictatorship."

"I'm not a dictator and damn it I love you. Nothing is going to happen to you. I'm here and I'll make sure that nothing happens to you but you've got to let me know where you are."

"So you can follow me? So you can micromanage everything I do? I need space, Doug! I won't get any when the baby is born. I'll never get this time back. I'll always be mom no matter how old our kid gets. But it's like you don't trust me to handle myself now, how will I ever even get to be mom for our kids?"

Doug grabbed Lisa's arms and pulled her close. "Damnit, Lisa, I—"

"Let go of me." She shrugged off his tight grip. "I'm going upstairs." Lisa turned and marched towards the stairs.

"No, you're not. We're finishing this argument now." He grabbed his tie from the coffee table and chased his bride. She was at the second step when he caught up to her and grabbed her hand. He spun her to and she fell into his arms. Holding her tight his hands rounded her behind and shoved her pink panties and grey joggers down her thighs. He squeezed her full cool bottom with a tight grip, sat her down on the third step and looked her directly in the eyes.

"You're not going anywhere."

The cool breeze in her inner thighs was soon warmed by his fingers planting themselves in her core. It was getting hot in the living room and her heart was beating faster.

"Oh, yes I am" She glared at him and shoved his hand away. She kicked off her clothes and lifted her bare bottom to sit on the fourth step. He threw the clothes across the floor, caught her right hand and tied it to railing.

"I expect you to let me know where you are."

"You're an asshole."

"And you love it." He knelt on the stairs and rounded his arms under her thighs, His face disappeared between them."

"Oh no. You're not doing this now." The increased sexual tension between them squashed the building anger. She firmly clasped the railing on the staircase and gyrated her hips upward. Her left hand grabbed clumps of his hair pressing him closer to her core.

He stopped; lifted his face to look up at her. She shoved his head back down towards her. He resisted.

"Beg."

"I will not."

"Then you will beg me to stop."

Placing his face back inside her thighs, he continued to devour his bride. Her heart was beating faster and her climax was eminent.

"Slow down. Slow down."

"Aaah"

He lowered her legs, stood up.

"I'm not done."

He dropped his jogging pants to the floor. He lowered his hand to stroke himself while staring her in the eyes. She panted, leaned back and placed her free hand inside of her thigh to cover the gate.

He closed the distance between their eyes covering her delicious lips with his. He parted her thighs and removed her hand.

She cooed and braced herself on the steps tipping her pelvis upward ready to receive more.

His fingers gripped the back of her spine, tilted her towards and him released the hooks her bra. He pulled the shirt over her head and the clothes rested on her right arm that was still tied to the banister.

His lips took turns between each breast. His mouth covered each nipple while his tongue traced the details firming the tissue with each soft lick.

"Ooh, tender." She moaned.

His fingers moved swiftly between her thighs raising and lowering to compliment her gyrations. He removed his hand and placed it on his manhood stroking it to feel if it was erect and ready for play.

It was.

Placing his fingers in her innermost thighs, he parted her lips and thrust himself into his woman for their personal pleasure, their connection on a physical and spiritual level.

"Aaah" she groaned.

"Yes." He moaned. Thrusting deeper and faster, he trembled, trying to hold back the climax building in him. She reached her peak singing to the heavens and he soon followed.

Shaking his head he lifted himself to a standing position, still panting, he untied his bride. "You're welcome." He smirked. "Glad to be of service."

Still catching her breath, she couldn't move from the stairs.

Damn.

Chapter 12

"I'm going upstairs for a while," Lisa said in-between pants of breath still gasping for air. She lifted herself from the steps leaving the rest of her clothes on the living room floor.

"Okay," Doug nodded and looked at her as she turned to go. His eyes gazed into hers pursing his lips to speak. Words formed but nothing but air released through them.

She slowly climbed the stairs feeling the pure exhaustion from their heated sexual encounter. There was more to Doug's controlling behavior than she realized and it extended to their sex life. She sat on her side of the bed.

"Lisa."

He was at the doorway and leaned in the frame. He partially dressed body was relaxed and his eyes downcast.

She stared into his eyes as he slowly approached her. He sat beside her, placed her hand in his lap and caressed her stomach.

"I'm sorry for yelling at you earlier." he said in a low soft tone. "I can't help it."

"I need my space." She intertwined her fingers in his. "If this is going to work, you have to give me space."

Doug nodded. "I hear you and heard you. I'll try but you've got to let me know what's going on."

"You can't be with me everywhere. I had a life before I met you." She said looking him directly in the eyes.

He stared back. "We're in this together. Let's both get some rest and go to Ray's later and get a few ties."

"Okay. I'll call Maya before we leave."

***

"Are you ready to go?"

Doug called out from the bottom of the stairs.

"Just a minute. I'm finishing my hair."

Doug smiled with pride when Lisa walked down the stairs in a red sweatshirt and grey jogging pants. She was a stunning woman, no matter what she wore.

"I called Maya," she said, putting on her green earrings. "She's expecting us."

"Great." Doug said as he was still gazing at his beautiful bride. He gathered her in his arms. "Forgiven?"

Lisa snickered, "No."

"What can I do to make it up to you?"

He placed soft gentle kisses behind her ear.

"I'll let you know." She waved him away. "We have to go."

***

Ray's New and Used Suits was a location not far from I-285 in Marietta. The parking lot was partially full and there were advertising signs in the windows for buy one get one-half off suits.

"I'll get that." Doug said as he pulled the door open for her.

Maya was busy at the cash register with four customers in line waiting to check out.

Lisa waved and Maya smiled.

"Let's look at the ties and talk to Maya when she's free."

"Sure."

Doug searched through the selection and chose a tie with a brown background. The colors were black, tan, and beige with a pattern print of tiny diamonds. It was a perfect match for the navy suit he was wearing to the Valentine's party.

"I like it." Lisa said, admiring the tie as he held it against his chest.

"Good."

They walked to the front of the store and Maya greeted them with a big smile.

"Hello newlywed cousins." She rounded the counter and gave Lisa a hug before turning to Doug. "You too, you get a hug also. You're family." She noticed the tie Doug was holding and her eyes crinkled as she looked at it then met his eyes. "We've got a new trend section with Fubu and Sean Jean if you prefer."

"Fubu?" Doug asked.

"For us by us." Maya said with a smile. "I know you aren't *us*, but many who aren't, like the style. Let me show you."

They followed Maya to the selection of trendy wear.

"A little young for me," he laughed.

"Oh, you've got to try on something." Maya begged. "You can't be married to my cousin and not wear something in style."

"I think that's a great idea." Lisa smirked. "I've got my own Vanilla Ice and I'm showing him off."

Doug's cheeks turned cherry. "Pick something. One outfit. No pictures."

"Deal." Maya said. She rummaged through the clothes and picked a large Fubu T-shirt and jeans. "Try this on."

Doug disappeared in the dressing room and Lisa wandered over to the suits to browse while waiting for him. She was startled by a man who approached her.

"Excuse me miss, how does this suit look on me?"

Startled, she looked at his dark eyes, thin face with a heavy moustache. He had on a light blue suit, yellow shirt and light brown shoes. She blinked her eyes a couple of times not knowing what to say and tried to give a tactful answer. "It's a unique color. Not everyone can pull that color off."

"Thanks miss. You got a man?"

"I'm married."

"—and that's my ring on her finger and my child in her belly."

Lisa whipped around to see Doug standing right behind her.

He took her hand and stared at the man in front of them.

She looked up at Doug, the blank expression on his face.

The man took a step back. "My bad. No harm, no foul." He walked away without incident.

She pulled Doug's sleeve. "What was that? I could have handled him myself."

"As my friend Greg would say, it's a man thing. Don't worry about it."

"Ugh" Lisa threw her hands up. "You're impossible."

Chapter 13

As Lisa was putting on her red tea length dress, with sequins streamed through the bodice, she glanced across the room at Doug. He was putting the cufflinks on his shirtsleeves while admiring himself in the mirror. They dressed many times together but today was special.

Their first Valentine's Day.

This time last year, she'd finished breaking up with a man that dated for two-years.

That time with Jaylon had convinced her that she never wanted to get married.

My how things change.

Lisa went to her closet and pulled out a black gift bag. She stood by her man, wrapped her arms around him, and handed him the gift.

"Happy Valentine's Day."

Startled by her surprise, he took the bag she offered.

"What's this?" He pulled the object out of the bag.

"A new laptop bag?" He turned it around and admired the leather. He zipped and unzipped the top of the bag to test the functionality.

"Yes."

He kissed her forehead. "Thanks. My current one was getting worn."

"I know it was. I found this for you while I was out with Corey."

She kissed him. "I really loved the flowers you sent to work. I'm so glad we're together."

"Me too," he searched his pockets, pulled out the tickets for the dance and placed them in his wallet.

Lisa stared in his eyes while Doug placed his hand on her abdomen.

"I love you in red," he half breathed the words to her, slipping his hand lower on her dress, warming places that made her gasp with delight.

"Be careful, Doug. That's how I got pregnant."

"Well, you can't get double pregnant."

"Do you want to skip the dance?" Lisa asked with a sly smile on her face.

Doug leaned over and gave her a short kiss. "No, I want to show off my lovely bride."

"Smooth talker, you."

***

They arrived at the main ballroom of the temple. Lisa followed Doug to their table. He pulled out her chair when they found their seats. The red and white carnation centerpieces were simple but stunning and she smiled across the table as she sat down.

Greg laughed at Doug's manners, shaking his head while his friend sat beside his wife and everyone settled at the table.

"How's my boy? You remember Bambi, right?"

"I do. This is my wife, Lisa." Doug shook Bambi's hand.

Lisa offered the other woman a smile.

"How are newlyweds?" Bambi asked. She brushed her blonde hair from her shoulders and reached for the cocktail in front of her.

"Just wonderful." Lisa answered.

"You both look it." Carter smiled at the couple, offering a nod to Doug in welcome.

Doug smiled and leaned close to his wife. "I'm getting a drink. Do you want anything?

"Shirley Temple."

Carter rose with Doug, "I'll go with you. I could use another too."

Greg followed them both, telling Bambi he'd bring her something too.

Lisa settled back in her chair and looked across the table.

Bambi had a tight forced smile on her face. "Greg said you went to Miami for your honeymoon?"

"We did. We had a great time." Lisa saw the forced smile on the woman's face turn to a horrified expression. Following Bambi's eyes to see what was going on; she spotted her sister and Ricky walking towards them.

Terri wore a long white gown with a fade of red that started from the knees. Ricky was in a black tuxedo. He held Terri's hand and strutted to the table as if he was the man of the hour. He stopped in his tracks five feet away, and his eyes widened as he stared at the table.

"Hi Terri, come sit next to me," Lisa called out.

"Sure thing." Terri pulled Ricky's hand and he reluctantly followed. His pace slower than hers as they moved around the table towards Lisa.

"Do you know Bambi? She's Greg's date." Lisa gestured in the blonde-haired woman's direction before turning to her and offered the rest of the introductions. "This is my sister, Terri, and her husband, Ricky."

Bambi's white face got paler. Ricky fumbled with something in his pocket barely acknowledged the other woman.

Terri didn't seem to notice anything was wrong.

"Don't we look alike?" Lisa asked Bambi. Lisa couldn't understand why this woman appeared to be nervous. Bambi twirled the fork in front of her and tried not to look across the table.

"Ahem," she placed her hand on her throat and massaged it. "Well now that you mention it. Yes, yes you do."

Ricky shot up out of his chair, "Terri, let's go dance." Ricky tugged his wife's hand and didn't give her a chance to sit down.

Lisa watched them go, wondering what just happened.

"It's a wonderful party." Bambi said as she struggled to make conversation.

"Yes, it is." Lisa answered.

Bambi's leg was shaking nervously and Lisa felt the vibrations from the table. Bambi reached in her clutch, pulled out her compact and checked her makeup. She slung her hair back off her shoulders and put her compact away.

Lisa shook observed Bambi and shook her head.

Greg could do much better than this woman.

What he picks is none of my concern.

An arm reached across her shoulder and placed a drink in front of her. "For you, my lovely wife."

Thank Goodness.

She turned her attention away from the other woman to her husband. She flashed him a smile and he grinned back.

Greg slid onto his chair next to Bambi. "Can you two lovebirds tone it down? You're making me look bad in front of my girl."

Doug laughed.

"That must have been some honeymoon. You're worse now than before you left. Come on Bambi, let's dance."

As Greg led Bambi away, Terri and Ricky arrived at the table. Terri's face had a frown so tight that there was no forcing a smile. Ricky was solemn. He moved his shoulders back and stiffened his spine.

Lisa wondered what that dickwad had said to her sister to dampen the mood between them

"Sis, come with me, I think I see someone we both know." Lisa said.

"Sure, I'll follow you."

***

"What the hell did he say to you?" Lisa demanded. The trip to the bathroom was detoured to a hallway where there weren't many guests.

"Forget it, Lisa. He's just an asshole and I never should have married him." Terri fought the tears Lisa saw forming at the corners of her eyes.

"You don't have to stay married to him. Get rid of that loser."

"It wasn't like this before. We can still work this out. We haven't been married a year yet!"

"Then get the damn thing annulled. You don't have any kids with him. He's not right for you. He's not right for anybody."

"Just let me work this out and focus on that controlling husband of yours. They start out sweet and then they sour. If you and Doug don't make it then we'll go to divorce court together."

Lisa inhaled to settle her anger. Terri didn't deserve to be disrespected and that was her big sister. There was nothing that Ricky could say or do now that would ever make Lisa like him.

"The family came for this big happy wedding. They expect newlyweds to have problems. Don't tell me that you're not having problems with Doug." Hurt and sadness were in Terri's eyes.

"We have problems but not like this. I haven't seen you happy at all with him. Every time I see you, it's before or after an argument with him. When is it going to get better for you? You're my sister. I love you."

Terri shook her head, backed away from Lisa, not wanting to prolong the pain of the conversation between them. "I've got to fix my makeup. He can't see me like this."

"Okay...better get moving before Doug sends out the search party for me."

At least that made her sister snigger a little. It was something to lighten her mood.

Chapter 14

Look at all these professional men and women who happen to be black.

I'm one of a handful of white men at this event.

I wonder what Lisa feels like when she comes to events like these and no one is like her.

The race thing opened a new territory of questions because of how it affected his social life now. Case law after case law, patient after patient, they all were numbers and statistics. They were the answers to why applied science and law did or did not work but nothing was personal until now.

"How was Miami?" Carter asked bringing Doug's thoughts into the present.

A smile widened across his face. "Great."

"Did you get to see the city or did you stay in your room?" teased Greg.

"Both," Doug responded with a wider grin. He took a sip of his vodka tonic. "Enjoyed it."

"Ah snap. My boy!" Greg leaned back in his chair and returned the wide grin. "Never going back."

"Nope." Doug's smiled. "Just Lisa."

"I'll never commit to a sistah," Greg said with a chuckle. "Too much damn drama."

"Stay with the white girls. Tame and lame. I'll take the drama."

"Ah that's cold. Marry one sistah and you got it all figured out. Call me in a few months after the baby is born. We could get a visa and move to Germany."

Doug raised his eyes to meet Greg's, "She would find me in Germany. I don't think there's anywhere on the planet that she couldn't find me."

Carter laughed, chuckled as he stood and motioned for Doug to come with him. "I have some frat brothers that I want you to meet. Greg, Ricky, are you coming?"

"Nah, I'm waiting for Terri. She should be back in a minute."

"I'll wait for Bambi too."

***

"This is Johnny Thomas." Carter introduced Doug to a middle-aged African-American man with dark glasses and a well-trimmed salt and pepper beard. "He's my frat brother and specializes in medical law."

Doug shook his hand. "Doug Bader. I'm also an attorney."

"Welcome. Are you enjoying the party?"

"Yes sir, I am."

Carter patted Johnny's shoulder and stepped away from the conversation, nodding to Doug that he was leaving.

"How did you hear about this event?"

"A friend of mine had tickets. I got married last week. We had a brief honeymoon and made it back in time to attend."

"Congratulations, Doug," he offered his hand to shake it again.

"Thanks, I have to check on her. She's expecting."

As Doug finished his statement, he felt a warm soft hand slip into his. He looked over and saw his new bride standing next to him. Quickly, he gave her a kiss on the cheek.

"This is my wife, Lisa."

"Nice to meet you. Are you also an attorney?" Johnny shifted his stance. He found a close place to set down his drink and extended his hand to greet her.

"No," she smiled. "That's his job. I'm a CPA. I work in his aunt's firm."

"Power couple." Johnny said with a wide smile. "I like it." Johnny reached into his pocket and pulled out his card.

Doug mimicked Johnny's gesture by pulling a card from the inside of his suitcoat to make the exchange.

"It's been a pleasure to talk with you. I'm going to find my own wife now. The four of us should get together for dinner."

"We'd like that."

Johnny walked away.

Doug read the services on his card. "Johnny's a medical attorney. I'll look him up later so I can ask his advice about starting a private practice."

"That's great. I hope he can point you in the right direction."

"Let's go back to the table. It may be time to eat." He took her hand and led her away.

Once they arrived at the table, Doug settled in his chair. He turned his head and caught a glimpse of Bambi's eyes. His face turned an ashen white and he squeezed Lisa's hand. She looked up at him and watched the pale expression on his face.

Same as in Miami.

He coughed and turned away from the table to catch his breath. Lisa offered him her drink.

"Sip slowly."

He took her water and swallowed. The choking slowed down. Taking deep breaths, he was almost back to feeling okay.

Once he felt he could string a few words together he whispered in her ear, "Can we go now?"

He looked at everyone's expression as he slowly came back to a normal breathing pattern. The meals were served to everyone and no one took a bite from their plate.

Lisa pushed back her chair. "I'm taking him home. I think he's coming down with something."

Good call Lisa, good call.

"I'm ready to go."

He didn't say a word and was thankful that she made their excuses to leave. Once arriving at the car, he sat in silence behind the wheel and stared out the window.

"Seriously. What's wrong? Are you okay?"

It took a moment for Doug to hear her. "No Lisa, I'm not okay. Bambi's pregnant and it's not Greg's."

Lisa sat motionless in the seat next to him.

Oh, shit. More questions are coming.

"Wait a minute, how do you know she's pregnant? You did this in Miami. What's going on, Doug?"

How in the hell do I explain this without creating a storm of questions?

He started the ignition. "I haven't told you everything. I didn't want you to think that I was crazy or weird. Since my parents passed away, I've been able to tell women that they're pregnant within days of conception. It started a month after the accident. A study partner of mine was finishing her last year in college. She came to the study group and talked about her boyfriend and his acceptance to law school. She was accepted to medical school far away from him. I innocently asked her who was going to take care of the baby and she was shocked.

She told me that she'd only found out that morning that she was pregnant and wondered how I knew. I didn't have an answer for her."

Lisa secured her seatbelt, placed her hand on the dashboard, turned to him and expressed her concern. "That's incredible, Doug."

"There's more. I thought it was a fluke. As I was training and working towards my doctorate, I had patients, and their family members that I told them they were pregnant. The most difficult women to tell were the teenage girls who were with their parents. I stood several feet away when I told them. Their parents became really angry."

"Wow. I would be angry too if my teenage daughter was pregnant."

He put the steering wheel in drive and backed out of the parking space.

"I got so good that the nurses on staff called me the human pregnancy test because I am one hundred percent accurate. I have never told a woman that she was pregnant and she wasn't. The more women I tell, the more insight I get. Like tonight, I not only knew that Bambi was pregnant but I also knew that it wasn't Greg's. I don't know who the baby belongs to but Greg is not the father." He shook his head. "I don't know how I'm going to tell Greg."

Lisa shrugged it off. "Let her tell him. She can't hide a pregnancy. It's not your place anyways, I don't' think it's ever really been your place. Think of all the weird looks you get every time you say that."

He pulled out of the parking lot into the street. They were at the traffic light at the end of the block. "I'm used to it. I just can't help it. When I get it, I must tell it. Aunt Mona taught me that years ago."

"Aunt Mona? Right! Yea, I know. She talks about dreams and spirits on occasion but hasn't gone into detail."

"There's more to it. You've been to her church a few times for events. I haven't taken you for message service."

"So, what does all of this have to do with you running across the country telling women they're pregnant?"

"It has everything to do with it. Aunt Mona was the black sheep of the family. She saw spirits when she was ten years old. The family thought she was insane and sent her to numerous counselors. When she was sixteen, she went to a psychic and they explained her dreams to her. She's been interested in it ever since."

Lisa crossed her swollen ankles. "Get to the point. What does this have to do with you?"

"My aunt and uncle were one of the founders of her church. When I was younger, I played a lot with my cousins and learned several spiritual lessons from them. My mother gave me permission to attend my aunt's church and my father being a strong Southern Baptist disagreed. My parents had lots of arguments over it but eventually my mother won. I do some message work but not like my Aunt Mona. She's really gifted but hides it to do her CPA work."

"Ugh" she sighed. "This isn't normal."

The light turned green and he pulled off.

"Who said I was normal?"

Chapter 15

"Mrs. O'Bader, are ye ready for the party we're having today" Doug turned his natural southern accent into a broken Irish drawl. "Ye best not over do it."

"I believe everything is ready. We might need more Coke, but otherwise should be fine."

"I'll get that. While I'm gone, will you please take a nap?"

"Are you telling me what to do again?" Lisa snapped at the surprised Doug. "Putting my breakfast in divider plates wasn't funny this morning."

"I'm looking out for you and the baby."

"The baby and I are tired of this game. Good idea. Go to the damn store and get out of the house for a while. The baby and I are going on a two-mile run. We're getting out of shape."

"You're pregnant," stated Doug as he placed his hands firmly on her shoulders. "Act like it and take care of yourself."

Lisa flung his arms off her. "I'm pregnant not an invalid with no brain and no common sense. Stop trying to think for me. Stop trying to control me. Stop it." She stormed out of the room.

Doug trailed her, caught up to her and blocked her from moving any further. "You're beautiful pregnant, not out of shape. Please don't go running. There are other exercises that you can do to stay in shape, or we can do them together."

She shoved him in the chest. "Why are you so impossible? Personal space. Personal space. Just give me some. It won't hurt you to do that."

Doug threw his hands up in surrender. "Okay, I'm out of the house for a little while. Is there anything else you want besides extra Cokes?"

She smiled. *How about a hatchet right through your temple?* "No, dear. Minimum two hours gone. Call a friend, get some coffee, buy a shirt, and just get out."

Doug glanced at his watch. "Okay, two hours and I'll be back. The party isn't until later today and I don't want you to lift or do anything extra."

She huffed and crossed her arms above her abdomen. "Don't call me either for two hours."

"What if you want something else from the store?"

"Then I'll call you." Lisa lifted her finger and pointed towards the garage. "Get the hell out."

Doug went to the table, grabbed his keys and exited out of the garage.

This marital thing was a challenge with the same arguments over and over again.

If she would listen to him, everything would go much smoother.

He pulled out his phone and gave Greg a call.

"Speak to me."

"Let's meet for coffee."

"Who the hell is this? I know it's not my married buddy Doug."

Doug laughed, "It is."

"I'm seeing you later and what the hell is this meet for coffee thing? Did you join AA?"

Greg always knew how to make light of any conversation whether or not it was serious.

"No AA. Lisa kicked me out of the house."

"Oh, hell naw. You do get to come back, right?"

"Yes, in a couple of hours. She thinks I'm smothering her."

"Naw, what would make her come up with that?" Greg said with a high note of sarcasm in his voice. "You keep a tight leash."

"I know."

"All right, where?"

"Starbucks and you know which one."

***

"One venti hot chocolate and a venti coffee," Doug ordered at the counter of Starbucks. His Wall Street Journal was under his arm and he had a few minutes to read the headlines before Greg joined him.

He grabbed their drinks and took a table by the window, waiting for his friend to show up.

Opening the paper, he read the same headline several times. His mind wasn't on the paper but the spitfire that he married. She was beautiful when she was angry and beautiful when she was happy. She wanted space and he wasn't willing to give her any.

She was *his* wife. His alone. No sharing. Completing his round of accomplishments. Money and family. She fulfilled his needs for a lifetime companion. Mother of their soon to be baby and mother of more to come.

"So, she kicked you out?"

Doug looked up at Greg who grinned and extended his hand.

Doug stood and reciprocated to seal a firm handshake.

Both men sat down.

"Not exactly. I've been ordered to go to the grocery store for a couple of hours and I'm not allowed to call her."

"Ouch." Greg laughed. "Sistah needs some me time. When the baby gets here both of y'all will get kicked out."

Doug picked up his hot chocolate and took a whiff before sipping. "She wouldn't kick the baby out. Just me."

"Yea, she would. "It's called 'Call the grandmother before I kill the baby and the baby daddy.' She'll call her mother first. I hope your Aunt Mona is on speed dial."

Doug laughed. "She is. Can I ask you something? Are black women always upset or is it Lisa and the pregnancy?"

"Aw hell naw. What happened to the excitement about being with a sistah? Keep the tame and lame white girls you said. Are you changing your mind?" Greg sipped his coffee.

"No." The word flowed out of his mouth without effort. Greg laughed.

"Get used to it. Black women are spicy. You *know* my mother; *you* know my relatives and you met Lisa's womenfolk. Get close to your father-in-law. He'll tell you how he handles his wife. Haven't they been married a long time?"

Doug nodded. "Thirty-five years. Do you know how old I'll be in thirty-five years?"

"Yeah. You'll be the old couple sitting on the couch in front of the TV arguing over what you get to watch and hoping the grandkids come by to see you."

Grandkids?

"I haven't thought that far ahead. Still coming later for the party?"

"I wouldn't miss it."

***

"Thanks for coming" Doug said to the men gathered Doug's man cave down in the game room.

All stood around the pool table waiting for the games to begin.

Doug and Greg were first up and racked the balls on the pool table. Doug took his shot and missed.

"Ow. Maybe next time."

"Let me ask you something," Darnell, Lisa's cousin, placed the butt of his q-stick on the ground and leaned against it. "You have this huge place, lots of money, nice car and all that. You could have any girl you want."

"You mean any white girl I want."

All the men laughed including Doug.

"Yeah. So, how in the hell did you end up with MY cousin?"

Doug glared over at Greg. "Ask him. He started it."

Greg backed away from the pool table, raised his hands and laughed in submission. "Am I ever going to live that down?"

Doug shook his head, "Nope."

He shook his head and turned to Darnell to answer. "I bet Doug that he couldn't get your cousin's number, and he couldn't."

"If he didn't get her number how did he end up with her?"

"Tell him," Greg waved to Harold to get his attention. "Tell him how Doug and Lisa got together."

Harold responded with a stoic expression. "Lisa jinxed his phone." His expression remained unchanged as the other men laughed at his response.

"How the hell did she do that?"

Doug responded, "Before I met Lisa, I had an address book full of phone numbers. I was on the cover of an Atlanta Magazine as Atlanta's most eligible bachelor. I had a minimum of five messages a day of women begging to go out with me. After your cousin explicitly told me that I was not getting her number, all the numbers in my address book were completely erased. I had no more phone messages. I couldn't get a date at all for weeks other than going out with Lisa. I've never had that happen to me."

"See, she did jinx his phone."

Everyone laughed.

Greg added. "I thought Harold was kidding. I tried to call dates for Doug. I couldn't get anybody to go out with him. Bambi got her friend Cheri to a date but by that time, Doug was so deep into Lisa that he didn't want to see anyone else anyways!"

Darnell laughed. "Does your phone work now?"

Doug answered, "It better not. I'm officially off the market."

***

"I think I'd better sit down," Lisa said exhaustedly. "I've been up since really early this morning. Doug warned me to take a nap and slow down. No one tell him I should've listened. He doesn't need to know he was right. I'll never live it down."

Ann brought Lisa a glass of orange juice. "My daughter is not used to anyone giving her directions, parents or husband." She smiled, ran her hand over Lisa's head. "He's right though, sweetie. You can't do what you normally do not until the baby gets here. Your body can't handle it right now."

Terri excused herself to take a call.

No one mentioned that her husband wasn't at the party, nor the expression on her face as she went outside.

"They aren't going to make it." Ann said, shaking her head. "I knew she should've never married that boy."

Lisa defended her sister, "Doug and I have our arguments too, Mom. Don't be so hard on Terri."

"That couple is getting divorced and I spent a lot of money getting them married. They should be in counseling to work things out first. If you and Doug are having problems this early, then you need to be in counseling too. That's what's wrong with this generation. You get married too fast and then wonder why it doesn't work. Your father and I—"

"Mom! Not everyone is perfect like Dad." Lisa looked toward the stairs by the kitchen.

Oh, shit here he comes

Not today.

Maybe two hours wasn't enough.

"Did you eat?"

Lisa waved Doug away, "Yes, I did."

"What did you have?" he asked.

"My day off, remember?"

"I just want to make sure you're still eating right."

Lisa spoke, gritting her teeth, "My dearest, Doug, if you don't walk away now, you're going to hear a pregnant woman scream to the top of her lungs and that's not good for the baby."

Doug looked around the kitchen at all the women waiting for his response. Embarrassed, he raised his hands and backed away. "I'll check on you later."

"You do that." She smiled.

Doug disappeared from the room.

"What was that about?" Ann asked.

"I've got this mom. I'm getting another helping of potatoes with pickles on top. Just make sure if he comes back that I don't shove him down the stairs."

Ann shook her head and pointed her finger at Lisa. "Counseling, you hear me? Counseling."

Chapter 16

"Greg has a lot of friends." Lisa commented while getting dressed for another party. Greg is hosting a party at the Dupree Country Club. It was the first time they'd be back there since their wedding.

"Yep." Doug replied. "His frat brother, Nate, passed the bar exam." Doug passed Lisa the invitation to read.

Between Doug and Greg, they both know enough attorneys to cover every area of law imaginable.

Nate Jones. That name sounds familiar.

Oh shit. I know him. That's Jaylon's brother. Jaylon may be there.

This will be a long evening if I have to introduce Doug to my ex.

"We should have a good time. What about that attorney from Valentine's Day? Have you heard from him yet?" she looked in the mirror and brushed on light lilac eyeshadow.

"Yeah, we're meeting for lunch next week. Both of our calendars were full so I hope neither one of us has to cancel."

"Are you ready to leave?" She threw her compact in her evening bag.

"I am. Let's go."

***

Lisa's burnt orange gown complimented her cocoa brown skin tone. She stood by Doug and looked around the room recognizing some of the guests from the Valentine's party as well as a few new faces.

Doug's smothering behavior normally bothered her, but tonight she didn't want him to leave her side. She held his hand tight until the baby forced her to release him.

"I'll be right back." She kissed him on the cheek and scurried to the ladies' room.

When she finished, she returned to the ballroom and scanned the space but didn't see anyone she specifically knew.

It looks like the coast is clear.

She gasped. Her feet were no longer on the floor and her body was lifted in the air from behind. The bear hug she received wasn't recognizable; neither was the musky aftershave from the man behind her.

Once her feet touched the ground, she turned with her fist drawn back, ready to fight, but she couldn't hit Jaylon.

Jaylon Jones.

Her ex.

Shit.

"How's my favorite girl?" He lunged forward to give her a kiss.

Lisa turned her head and it landed on her cheek. She shoved him away from her, fists still clenched as he crowded her against the wall. "I wouldn't try that again. I have a very jealous husband and I don't want to spend all night explaining you to him." She stepped back to keep her distance from his unwanted affection.

Jaylon's eyes widened with surprise. "I didn't know you were married." He looked down at her rounded abdomen. "And pregnant!"

She smirked "I am pregnant."

He frowned at her. "You didn't want to stay home and have any of my babies."

Lisa scowled. "Not a chance, Jaylon. We couldn't get along and you didn't have time for me."

I can't believe this asshole picked me up.

If he does that again he won't have to worry about Doug.

Where the hell is Doug? I normally can't take a five-minute crap without him wanting a test sample to see what I've eaten.

Jaylon moved closer to her. "I called you several times. I wanted—" Jaylon looked up and stepped back.

Lisa felt heavy breathing over her shoulder. Arms folded around her abdomen, pulling her in.

She looked behind her into Doug's icy blue eyes.

It's about damn time you showed up.

Lisa smiled, not looking back at the other man. "Jaylon, this is my husband, Doug Bader."

Doug bent down to give her a kiss. She welcomed him in and took pleasure in his touch.

"This man is your husband!" Jaylon said in disbelief.

"He is," she continued to smile. "A lot has happened since we last spoke." Lisa placed her hands over Doug's resting on her stomach.

"I didn't think that you would get married so soon after we broke up."

Lisa halted any further conversation, "It's nice to see you again, Jaylon. My husband and I have to go."

Lisa removed Doug's hands from her abdomen and pulled him to walk away. She couldn't get away from the other man fast enough and hoped that he wasn't following.

"What was that about?" Doug asked.

How much does he need to know? My private life has always been private. We're married and Jaylon is unimportant. But maybe if I open up, he'll be more willing to open up to me…

"Ex-boyfriend and no one important to me." Lisa continued to walk away with Doug's hand in hers.

He pulled her to a stop. "I think I deserve an explanation, Lisa."

"We're at a party, having a good time. There's nothing to explain." Lisa knew that dismissing this discussion would cause an argument and this wasn't the place to have one.

"Now, Lisa. Tell me something, now." Doug's cheeks hollowed and his face flushed.

Not the way she wanted to spend the evening at this posh event.

She folded her arms across her chest. "Jaylon and I were seeing each other for two years and it finally ended six months before I met you. I don't want to discuss Jaylon any further, especially not in this setting. I would prefer to drop the entire conversation."

Doug's icy cold stare sent a slight chill up her arm. He jerked her hand and pulled him beside her. The stoic angry look remained on his face.

"We'll continue this later, Mrs. Bader."

"Yes, Mr. Bader."

Well hell...

There were enough arguments between them without dragging up her past relationships. More questions were coming about Jaylon and she preferred that his legacy remain dead and buried.

Damnit.

***

"I want to talk about it." Doug asked from behind the wheel of the car. They left thirty minutes prior to the event closing for the evening. "I want to know if I should be worried about more men from your past showing up like assholes."

"Oh, no," Lisa pointed her finger at him, "we're not having this argument. There's a reason why I haven't discussed my dating history with you. You can't handle it." Lisa kicked her pumps off and wiggled her toes. Her feet were swollen from standing too long.

"You refuse to talk about it every time I bring this up. We're married. We're supposed to be honest with each other."

Lisa flounced back in her seat and crossed her arms. "Because you're so open with me?"

"This isn't about me, Lisa. We're having the discussion now." Doug's fingers gripped the steering wheel as if it were trying to get away.

"Hell no."

"You can't hide everything."

She thought about his statement. She expected him to be forthcoming with her, and he wasn't, and neither was she.

Maybe it wasn't just his fault.

If they were not open with each other, they could end up like Terri and Ricky.

She relaxed her arms and laid her hands in her lap. "Fine, but this will be the only discussion about Jaylon." She pursed her lips and waited for Doug to nod his agreement. "I met him in Atlanta through a mutual friend. As I said, we dated for about two years. I traveled quite a bit so I didn't have much time for him. We would try to see each other when I was in town but our schedules rarely matched. When we did see or talk to each other, we argued constantly about everything."

"What did you argue about?" Doug asked.

"He wanted me to give up traveling soccer and be with him. He never said that he wanted a commitment, he just expected me to give up my goals and dreams. He's an attorney at his father's law practice. Nate's his brother. You never said the last name so I didn't make the connection until you handed me the invitation." She shook her head. "Everyone thought that we would get married. I would've never fit into that family."

"I saw him kiss you," Doug said.

"Did you see me shove him away?"

"No."

"I'm not leaving you for that lying cheating bastard. I'm not in love him." Lisa pulled Doug's hand and placed it on her abdomen. "Do you feel this?"

Doug looked at Lisa then back at the road.

"I love you. I married you. I would never do this for Jaylon."

"Why not? Why didn't you work out? Just because you don't fit in his family can't be the only reason. I don't fit into your family."

"I knew if I married him that it would end in divorce. It just never worked. We spent a lot of time together and we didn't know each other at all. I just couldn't see spending the rest of my life with him. We were complete opposites. He wanted a wife at home. I wanted to travel. He wanted kids. I didn't. He wanted us to attend his church and I wasn't fond of his church. The last thing that I wanted to do was to marry a know-it-all attorney."

He pondered over her explanation.

Although they had differences, they weren't complete opposites.

"Seems to me that you did just that, Lisa, except I'm white and he's black."

"I don't love him! You're not him. Two years down the drain. Why are we talking about this?"

"We're talking about this because you're keeping secrets. I need to know what's going on. We have enough societal pressures to deal with. Ex-boyfriends shouldn't be an issue.

"He's only an issue because you're making him one. This discussion is closed." Lisa folded her arms, reclined her chair and closed her eyes.

Doug looked through the windshield at the people on the sidewalk walking around the streets of Atlanta. He allowed her a moment to cool her anger.

She opened her eyes and turned to him. The streetlights reflected in her eyes. She reached for his hand.

"Jaylon's not important." Her eyes softened and voice mellowed. "The thought of never crossed my mind once we met. It was a closed part of my past."

He squeezed her hand and returned his hand to the steering wheel.

She took a deep breath and continued, "Our relationship happened so fast. Once I moved in with you, I knew in five days that you and I would be together and I'd be having your children."

He grinned. "I considered getting a vasectomy. If we met a couple of years later, there would be no children. Since I met you, I had to rethink my values about starting a family."

She laughed "So what changed your mind?" she patted her stomach."

He chuckled with her. "You did. My single life was over and fatherhood was eminent."

"I still think about the night we got engaged. I watched the expression on your face. I think you knew right then that I was pregnant."

Doug had a faraway look in his eyes. He was searching for what to say and she waited for his answer. "You're right. I felt our lives were about to change again. I couldn't tell you what I was feeling. I thought it was purely a release of passion. It was our first time together and we'd just gotten engaged."

"When did you know that we would be together?"

"The night we met in the restaurant."

Chapter 17

"Which law firm is cosponsoring this event?"

"Smith Wheatley. This fundraiser has a twenty-year history. The winner keeps the original trophy. Whitman Stacks has won seven times in the last twenty years. Smith Wheatley attorneys are difficult to beat." Doug finished shaving and combed his hair.

Lisa was dressed and waiting for him to finish. "Calm down. You'll do just fine,"

He was brushing his teeth scrubbing furiously in a circular motion. "I don't want to mess up. Everyone is counting on me and Harold."

"Both of you put in a lot of practice. You'll do fine. The children's charity will be thankful for whatever monies are raised."

"I'm sure they will."

His response echoed in the bathroom, which made it difficult for Lisa to hear him.

"What did you say?" she asked.

Doug walked to the doorway. "I'm sure they will. The charities will be thankful."

"This will be fun to see the kids run the program. How cool is that?"

Doug laughed, "Very." Now the dental floss was moving rapidly through his molars.

How much dental floss can he use in a week? We should buy it wholesale and save money.

Doug came out of the bathroom and stood before her. "We need the win. I'm tired of Jeff Wheatley bragging on himself. I'm a sharper attorney and he knows it."

"Come feel the baby move. That should get you to relax."

Doug finished flossing and leaned Lisa back on the bed hugging her round body and feeling some slight movement.

He kissed her on the neck and jumped up. "Let me get my stethoscope so I can hear my baby's heart."

"Don't you dare. You'll be late. Let's go before I have to go to the bathroom again."

***

When they arrived at Dupree Country Club, there were signs all over the grounds directing traffic to the fundraiser. Making their way to the entrance, they received an itinerary with the schedule of events.

"The law bee is first. Hurry and find your team."

"I'm not leaving you yet." He smiled and kissed her cheek.

"I'm fine. Terri will be here soon. Go."

Lisa took a seat in the Mirage Room, which had a continental breakfast for the guests. She read over her itinerary.

Law bee, spelling bee, trivia, family feud.

Someone sat down next to her and she looked up at the familiar face.

"Hi, Lisa."

"It's good to see you, Hannah. You look like you're due any day now."

Hannah laughed. "I'm only eight months pregnant. How's your pregnancy coming along?"

"Doug's pregnancy is coming along fine. He has planned my daily activities as well as all my meals. It's wonderful…"

Hannah laughed at Lisa's sarcasm. "I thought Harold was kidding. I didn't know Doug was doing all of that."

"I hope someone takes a picture of the baby at the hospital. I don't know how much I will get to hold it. He's very into this child."

"How does that make you feel?"

"Overwhelmed, but I know he is doing everything out of love for me and our baby. Both families are very excited."

"I'm excited for you. Did you hear that Whitman Stacks sold the most tickets? Harold was elated." Hannah brushed her hands across her abdomen, which started moving as soon as she touched it. "I can't wait until the little man gets here."

Lisa stood up from her seat and looked back at Hannah. "I'm getting a muffin. Do you want one or more?"

"Oh no," she sighed, "I'm full. Harold and I ate breakfast before we came."

Lisa laughed. "Me and Doug too, but I'm still getting a muffin. I'll be right back."

She walked over to the table with several coffee pots and saw a familiar face.

Navy blue shirt and tie, Greg smiled when he noticed her standing next to him. "You look lovely, Lisa. How's everything going? I haven't talked to Doug in a while. How's he doing?"

"Between the baby and this fundraiser, he's been working overtime."

Greg laughed, poured a cup of coffee and offered it to her. "Is he still ordering all of your meals?"

Lisa accepted the cup and took a sip before she spoke. "I think you know the answer to that. This will be the healthiest baby that I have ever seen. I'm afraid the baby will come out talking medical mumbo jumbo with the way the father talks."

Greg offered her a napkin and she accepted. "That's Doug. Look, I have to go. He doesn't allow any men to talk to you long. I'm not trying to get on his bad side. Excuse me. I'll talk to you soon."

Lisa chuckled. "He doesn't let anyone talk to me long. Take care."

Greg winked and walked away. She placed her lips on the rim of the cup for another sip and almost choked midstream. She caught a glimpse of Jaylon fast approaching.

No Doug to rescue her this time.

Oh shit.

I haven't seen him in months and now twice in the last six weeks.

"Lisa Dunbar, we didn't have a chance to talk the last time we spoke."

"Pretty sure that's what speaking is, Jaylon." She placed her cup back into her saucer and glared at him. "It's now Lisa Bader and there's nothing else to talk about. I'm married and happy and it has nothing to do with you." Lisa looked at him proudly as she patted her very pregnant stomach.

Jaylon huffed, "Why did you marry a white guy? Did I turn you off from all brothers?"

"My marriage to Doug has nothing to do with you or what color his skin is," she snapped. "I don't have the time or desire to tell you how Doug and I got together."

"I called you several times and you never returned my calls."

"We were done, Jaylon. Take a hint. Haven't you found someone else?" Her lips tightened and she looked around the room.

"Yes, I've dated off and on. We never closed out our relationship."

Oh, you closed it the minute I found that hussy's panties under your bed.

Lisa scanned the room and caught Greg's eye. He acknowledged her by nodding. He wrapped up his conversation, walked over to Lisa, and stood beside her.

"Jay." He nodded to the other man. "Lisa, are you ok? Everything is about to start soon."

Jaylon looked Lisa directly in her eyes. "This discussion isn't over."

She half shouted, "I am six months pregnant with my husband's baby. This conversation is long over." Lisa stormed off leaving Jaylon standing with Greg.

"Why don't you leave that sister alone? What are you going to do with a pregnant married woman?"

Jaylon answered, "I don't know why I lost it. The memories came back quickly. I thought Lisa and I would have married by now but her soccer career came first. Now she's married and having a baby. She never allowed me the chance to make her happy."

Greg shook his head. "I would suggest that you stay away from Lisa. Doug is deep into her and she is deep into him. If he weren't busy with the fundraiser, he would've been standing right behind her. Doug doesn't let Lisa out of his sight."

"I met him at Nate's party. I don't know why in the hell she married that white guy."

"I had something to do with their introduction. I was also his best man at their wedding."

Jaylon looked alarmed. "So, you know her husband?"

"He's been my best friend since high school. Let's join the group and watch the spelling bee."

* * *

Feeling the fire rage through her body, Lisa marched to the bathroom to calm her nerves. That man knew how to push every hot button to make her angry.

Taking a cool paper towel, she dabbed her face.

Why did I let that asshole get to me like this?

He had a lot of nerve to march his lying cheating ass over to me.

It's a good thing I've got Doug.

I love Doug.

"I love Doug," she said aloud and smiled at her reflection in the mirror. Taking a deep breath, she closed her eyes and slowly exhaled.

The door opened to the bathroom and, much to her surprise, Terri walked in.

"I saw Jaylon talking to you. Are you okay?"

"I'm fine, Terri. I hope he doesn't cause any problems. I don't want Doug to be upset." She threw her paper towel in the trash.

"I don't want *you* to be upset. I'm worried about you."

"I'm pregnant and emotional. I just forgot that he was an attorney and could be at this event. Isn't there someone that you can introduce him to occupy his time? He doesn't bother me when he's dating."

Terri placed her hand on her hip, "I don't know any woman that could put up with that. I don't know how you did it."

Lisa sighed, "I thought I was in love with him at the time. It just didn't work. I love Doug. That's the difference."

Terri's face was grim "From one controlling man to another. Only difference, Doug's got more cash."

"Stop it, Terri," Lisa snapped.

"You said that you would never have children. Soccer was your life."

"So? I changed my mind. I'm allowed to do that, Terri. Don't you and Ricky want children?"

"As much as he and I are arguing, never with him."

"Let's get back to the fundraiser. I know Doug will be looking for me in the audience."

Chapter 18

"Whitman Stacks is this year's winner of the Dupree Country Club Children's fundraiser"

Doug's face beamed with pride as he stood by Mr. Whitman to accept the trophy. He looked through the sea of faces after shaking his boss' hand, searching for Lisa and spotting her next to her sister before raising the trophy high with both hands for everyone to see.

The crowd cheered.

He winked at her and she blew back a kiss.

It was a great day and winning made it surreal.

He shook Mr. Whitman's hand again. "I'm taking my wife home. It's been a long day for her."

"Good job. I'm glad you're with the firm."

"Thank you." Doug made his way through the crowd to Lisa. He pulled her in for a tight kiss.

"Congratulations." Lisa smiled and gazed into his eyes. "Well done."

"Let's get out of here or we'll be here all night."

***

Lisa was sleeping on the couch when she heard Doug's voice. The smell of garlic and herbs was enough to stir her from her rest. She blinked a couple of times and he was standing over her.

"I have dinner ready if you're hungry. Are you hungry?"

Lisa yawned and stretched and propped herself up. "I'm starved. I want to talk to you first."

She took him by the hand and pulled him down next to her. "Jaylon approached me today at the fundraiser. I wanted to tell you first before anyone said anything."

His nose flared and cheeks tightened. "What did he say to you? I don't want you upset."

"Nothing important; he's just curious about our marriage."

He leaned over to her placing his hand under her chin tilting it to face him. "I don't want you talking to him."

She pursed her lips and stared him directly in the eyes. "I don't want to talk to him."

By the expression on his face, she didn't think he was convinced.

"Fine," he released her chin but his response was terse. She sighed, not wanting to deal with his irrationality again.

"I'm also worried about Terri. She and Ricky are fighting more and more." Lisa covered her legs with the blanket and positioned herself to lay nestled next him.

He placed his hand over her stomach to comfort her. "Fighting is normal in a marriage so you shouldn't worry."

"I'm worried because we're fighting more and more. You are trying to control everything and this can't work."

"I'm not. Let's get you fed. It's been a long day and we can discuss this later." Doug stood up and extended his hand to pull Lisa from the couch.

She waved it away. "We're talking now! Sit." She pointed next to her and waited for him to plop back on the couch. "We're not skirting this issue. It's time to really talk."

"I'm listening."

"Your control is escalating to the point where I can't breathe. I can't stay in this marriage if you're going to follow me everywhere, tell me what to eat, come shopping with me, and not let me have time to myself. You had a life before me so live it. Greg said he hasn't seen you in a while either."

Doug rubbed his hands over his knees. "So, you want me to hang out in the singles' bars with Greg on the weekends and do the things I did before we got married?"

Lisa shouted, "NO! You know what I'm talking about. I have girlfriends that I want to talk to on the phone without you listening behind the door. I have friends I'd like to have dinner with and catch up on news. I have soccer business to attend to without you in my ear giving me second judgements. When I want your opinion, I'll ask."

Doug glared back at her, "The problem is that you are so independent that you don't ask. We're doing this together. You want to make all decisions without me."

"You don't let me make any all because I'm the one that's pregnant."

"I'm the father, Lisa and I'm a doctor. I know what I'm talking about and you won't listen to me." His eyes turned steel blue as he stared at her.

Lisa pursed her lips, "The point is that the changes are happening to me. I'm not a textbook. I need time to make my decisions on what's good for me and the baby without you always interfering."

"I'm not interfering, I'm helping." He couldn't understand why Lisa didn't allow him to make decisions about her and the baby without it being a big argument.

She gritted her teeth and clenched her hands beneath the blanket. "Do you think we need counseling, counselor?"

"Do you?"

"I can't stay in this marriage if we continue to argue like this."

Doug stood up. He gazed into the anger and hurt in her eyes.

"I'll make a call to Dr. Zwinger."

Chapter 19

"Welcome Doug and Lisa. My partner and I thoroughly enjoyed your wedding and thank you for inviting us to attend."

Lisa said, "It was our pleasure and privilege to have the both of you at our wedding."

Doug nodded in agreement.

"Are you ready for your session?"

"Sure."

"Now that you've had a few months together, are there any observations that you want to share with each other?"

"I'll go first." Doug said, "Lisa and I have separate bathrooms. She can't stand the toilet seat up."

Dr. Zwinger put his pen down on his paper and laughed. "I hear that often. That can be a problem for a woman. What else?"

"Since my mother passed away, I've never lived with a female. Lisa has a large accumulation of stuff. We're still sorting through it."

Lisa chuckled.

"Please continue, Lisa you'll have your say next."

"We have very different tastes in music. I've never heard of some of the songs that she listens to. Also, Lisa snores at night. I think a lot of that has to do with the baby."

Lisa laughed some more.

"Lisa, what are your observations of Doug?"

"We agree on the bathrooms, I do have a lot of things. It seems like a lot because we are combining households. It's true that Doug and I have very different tastes in music. I can't defend myself on the snoring. Sorry, Doug. That runs in the family."

Lisa leaned back on the couch and shifted into a comfortable position. "Doug is a fitness fanatic and is always on the treadmill. He's an avid reader especially medical and legal journals. He brushes his teeth at least three times a day. I may buy stock in toothpaste."

Doug chuckled.

"Well let's continue. Have you filled out the questionnaire that I requested for our visit?"

"Yes." Lisa said

"I did." Doug nodded.

"This exercise is to get couples to talk to each other about matters that can arise during a marriage. We aren't going over all of them but I will pick out a few of them to discuss during our session. Are you ready?"

They both nodded.

"It is your marriage and the both of you are responsible for being honest with each other. Dishonesty with each other can bring unnecessary strife in a marriage." Dr. Zwinger picked up his notepad and clicked his pen. "We're going to question seven. Why did you commit your life to this person in marriage? Who would like to go first?"

Lisa said, "I will. I love Doug. He complements my personality. I try to take a broad look at life and he pays attention to all the details. He is very active socially and so am I. We are spiritually connected." Lisa and Doug held hands and smiled at each other.

"Doug?" asked Dr. Zwinger.

"Making a commitment of any kind is very difficult for me. When I met Lisa, I tried to avoid the inevitable. Lisa knows more about me that any other person that I've ever met in the short time that we've been together. I can't imagine spending the rest of my life without her."

Lisa's cheeks turned a cherry brown color and Doug squeezed her hand.

Have you had a discussion on your cultural differences?"

"We are beginning to have those discussions. It didn't come up when we first started seeing each other. These issues were never forefront in my life. I was aware of them but not a part of them."

Lisa released Doug's hand. "I told him that these issues are an everyday part of my life as a minority. When the baby comes, Doug and I both will be answering questions from an inquisitive public."

Dr. Zwinger responded, "I can recommend books on that topic if you want. I'll look up the names of books and authors and send a list of recommended readings to you."

Dr. Zwinger jotted down a few more notes, clicked his pen and looked at the couple. "Have your families accepted the fact that you are married to a person of a different culture?"

"My family likes Doug. He gets ownership of all the white names like, vanilla, saltine, snowflake, Wonder bread, reverse Oreo… The list continues."

"Hmm." Dr. Zwinger motioned for Doug to answer. "How does that affect you?"

"It bothered me at first but I had lunch with Lisa's mother and she explained that to be accepted in her family, you got teased. I'm not allowed to repeat what they call her. I'm staying on good terms with my mother-in-law."

Lisa laughed. "Yes, my family does pick on each other." Doug chuckled too.

"And your family, Doug? How do they feel about your marriage to Lisa? This is the south. Interracial families do face extra challenges."

Doug said, "My brother Todd is taking exception to the marriage but supported us by taking part in our wedding. I've had lots of questions from persons other than my family."

"What types of questions?" Dr. Zwinger asked.

"Why would I marry someone black? Why are you marrying her so fast? Did you think about the racial differences? Did you think of how this would affect your children? I'm tired of the bullshit. This is my wife and I love her."

"I love you too."

***

"Well that wasn't too bad." Doug said about Dr. Zwinger's visit as they approached the car to go home.

"We still didn't air out all of the dirty laundry." Lisa said.

"Did you think we would resolve this in one visit? Issues like ours will take a while to sort out."

"What if we can't sort this out?"

Doug's arms wrapped her close. "I know an excellent divorce attorney." He brushed his lips against her ear and followed up with a kiss.

"Not funny." She frowned.

"Lighten up, Lisa."

He opened the door and she slid into her seat. She sighed and watched him come around the front of the car to take the driver's side. He got in and started the ignition.

"By the way," she said, "why do you always have to drive? I can drive. I've had a license since I was sixteen."

He turned off the ignition, pulled out the key, jingled the keyring and handed the keys to her. "I don't. You want to drive, drive." He waited for her to take his offering. "If a thirty-minute drive back to our residence is going to make you happy, drive."

Lisa took the keys and hauled herself out of her seat to exchange places with him. He watched her as she settled behind the steering wheel and he buckled himself in.

She stared out of the windshield. She let out a loud wail and tears fell down her cheeks.

"Lisa?"

She wiped a few of her tears. "I'm fine. It's just the hormones. Let it go, okay?"

He reached under the seat, pulled out a box of tissues and handed them to her. She pulled out a few and dabbed her face taking deep breaths to calm down.

His phone rang. "I don't have to get that."

"Get it," she sniffled, "It may be important."

Doug sighed and answered. He sat in silence listening to the excited voice yelling at him over the line, a smile crossing his face though Lisa still sat sniffling behind the wheel. "That's great, Harold. Congratulations. When can you have visitors?"

He hung up the phone and Lisa looked at him, waiting.

"They had the baby. A boy. James David Cole."

"That's wonderful! How's Hannah doing?"

"Great. They said it would be fine to stop by if you're feeling up to it."

The tears had stopped and she looked okay to him. Maybe it was just the hormones like she said. He'd seen enough of that when he was still practicing medicine but he was worried. He didn't want her stressed.

Still, maybe…

"Perfect. But we're stopping for food on the way."

"I'm at your mercy, driver. Just remember the rules."

She growled at him and he laughed at her reaction.

She didn't laugh back.

Chapter 20

"Are you ready" Doug asked and wrapped his arms around Lisa's waist. "I love you in red. It should be your entire closet."

Lisa placed her fingers on his behind and squeezed. "I love you too,"

"Mark's estate isn't far from here. We should get there in about twenty minutes."

"Ooh," she breathed as he let her up for air. "Let's skip the damn party." She placed her red manicured nails on his lips and smeared her lipstick across them.

Doug lifted his hand and placed her fingers in his bending her fingers downward to place a kiss on her smooth brown skin. "We must make an appearance."

"Let's go and come back early then."

***

There were about a hundred guests expected at this posh and private affair. A dark curly haired man greeted them as they approached the entrance to the gate. Doug rolled down his window.

"Invitation please."

Doug reached in his left pocket to pull out his personal invite. The man looked over his clipboard and handed his invitation back to him.

"This way, you may enter."

Driving up to the front of the two-pillar estate, a man dressed in a red coat greeted him at the driver's side window.

"Valet sir."

Another man opened the car door for Lisa and she stepped out and waited for Doug to finish with the valet. He extended his hand to take hers, and they walked up the flight of steps to the entranceway.

"Welcome. I'm Margaret, your hostess for the evening. The guests are in the great room."

"Thank you." They followed the woman with "Addie" on her nametag.

Doug leaned over and whispered to her. "Are you ready to have some fun? We seem to stir a lot of conversation with the older guests."

"Oh, we certainly do." grinned Lisa. She held his hand tight. "I bet they're saying I'm glad that's not my son married to that black woman."

Doug snickered. "Behave, at least until we get home."

"Why, Mr. Bader," Lisa said in her most Southern belle twang that she could muster, "I do believe you are incorrigible."

Doug laughed and the joy in his face faded to something stern and serious. Lisa looked followed his stare.

Jaylon.

I didn't think Mark Steward knew any black people.

Is he starting his own damn affirmative action plan?

And what the hell! Who does he have on his arm?

That woman looks just like me!

Jaylon was dressed in his black-tie attire. His companion was very fair in complexion with similar features to Lisa. His companion's hair was a little longer and she was a few sizes larger. She held on to Jaylon's arm and looked at him with admiration.

Doug tightened his grip on Lisa's hand and she responded to by giving him a kiss.

"Welcome, Doug" Mark said breaking the bonding moment between them. "It's good to see you too, Lisa."

"How's Judith?"

"She's wonderful. She's planning the next party for Valentine's Day. I need to borrow your husband for a minute. Chad Wheatley wants to meet him."

"I'll be back in a moment."

Lisa noticed the bubbling fountain of golden punch and wandered her way over to pick up a long-stemmed glass. The water was next to it and she filled her glass with it before moving to her table.

She arrived at the same time as Jaylon's brother, Nate.

"Hi Lisa, it's good to see you. Are you enjoying the evening?" Nate extended his hand.

"Yes sir, I am."

"When's the baby due?"

She smiled. "Not soon enough."

Nate offered her a pink napkin. "My brother has never gotten over you. I was sure the two of you were going to get married."

"Not a chance. You and I both know he kept other women and I wasn't putting up with it."

Nate nodded in agreement and took a few steps away from the table. "I just wanted to speak. You have a lovely evening."

Nate walked away leaving Lisa to scan the room. She didn't see Doug at first but noticed him walking towards another room. He glanced her way but kept walking.

Where the hell is he going?

Lisa took a sip of her water and placed it back on the table to follow him. He was in the living room walking over to Jaylon.

Oh shit.

Doug knows not to start a scene here.

I've got to see what he's going to say.

"So, you're Lisa." Jaylon's date blocked her path.

"Yes ma'am, how are you? Have we met?" Lisa placed her hands on her hips and was ready for any action that may transpire.

"I'm here with Jaylon. I'm Taquanda. Stay away from my man." Her nose flared with anger.

Lisa fired back. "I don't want your man. Do you see the blonde talking to him?"

Taquanda answered, "Yes, ma'am, I do."

"That's my husband. Do you see this stomach?" Lisa patted her stomach and watched her eyes widen with surprise. "This is our baby that's coming."

Taquanda let out a deep sigh of relief. "You're married to a white guy!"

Lisa rolled her eyes. "My husband's name is Doug. I love him very much. How long have you been seeing Jaylon?"

"I've been seeing him for the last two years."

That was the same time he was with her!

This was the hussy who left her nasty drawers under his nightstand.

"Really!"

Taquanda said, "I knew about you. I was happy when it ended. I still haven't been able to get him to commit to me because he's still in love with you."

"I have no interest in Jaylon. You have to take care of that yourself. I want to see what he's telling my husband. Why don't you come with me?"

Lisa and Taquanda approached the pair in mid conversation.

"Stay away from Lisa. We just got married."

"You seem threatened. Are you afraid that she will walk out on you and come back to me?"

"She would never do that. I know Lisa."

Lisa quickly took Doug's hand and gave him a kiss. He smiled at her and then looked at Taquanda. Doug's eyes glazed and his right ear twitched. Lisa felt a tingling sensation from his fingers. The expression on his face looked like the one she saw with Bambi and the hotel clerk.

Not again.

She's not.

She is!

Lisa looked at Doug waiting for the bombshell to drop.

Doug smiled at Jaylon, which highly annoyed him.

"What are you smiling about?" Jaylon asked.

"You're about to become a father." Doug smirked.

Taquanda looked at Lisa and Doug with a horrified expression.

"What are you talking about?" Jaylon asked.

"Ask the woman who's in love with you. If I were you, I would beg her forgiveness and marry her right away; otherwise you'll never see your baby."

Lisa held Doug's hand tightly. Taquanda looked up at Jaylon.

His head jerked back and his jaw tightened. "You don't know what you're talking about. I don't have any children and no one's pregnant." Jaylon turned to Taquanda and asked. "What's wrong with you?"

Taquanda's face turned serious. She turned on her heels and stormed off. Lisa felt the anger rise in her chest.

He's an asshole but she didn't deserve that.

"This is exactly why I never could have married you, Jaylon. Taquanda is in love with you and she is pregnant." Lisa rushed off to go find the other woman and left Jaylon standing with Doug.

What a prick?

I'm so glad that it's over between us.

She heard sobbing in a room next to the laundry. She knocked.

"Taquanda. It's Lisa. Let's talk."

"Go away." She sniffled through the door. "I can handle my own business."

Lisa knocked again. "I know you're upset. He's a jerk and that was mean."

Lisa felt a tap on her arm. It was Jaylon. "I got this."

Lisa stepped back.

He squared himself in front of the door and called out in a low and somber voice. "I'm a jackass. Let's talk."

The latch unhitched and the door opened slowly. Taquanda's eyes were puffy and she continued to dab the tears that smeared her makeup.

Lisa turned to find Doug standing right behind her. They walked away and stood by the golden punch bowl. Lisa looked up into Doug's eyes and smiled. "I'm glad you told Jaylon that Taquanda was pregnant."

He returned the smile. "I had personal motives. I had to get rid of him."

"You didn't have to get rid of him. I wasn't going anywhere." Doug pulled Lisa close and gave her a kiss.

"I wasn't taking any chances with that."

Chapter 21

"Nooooo."

Shaken from his slumber, Doug rolled away from Lisa and looked at the digital clock. It was 4:00 a.m. The same dream, the same woman and the same result. She was gone and never to return.

He slid out of bed and walked into the bathroom closing the door to release his thoughts.

This can't be happening.

It's got to stop.

He looked in the mirror and brushed his hand through his hair wondering if he was ever going to release Tiffany. It had been fifteen years and it still felt as if she died yesterday.

He was married now.

Why couldn't he move on?

Turning out the light in the bathroom, he climbed back into the bed with Lisa.

He was getting accustomed to the rhythmic snoring sound she made through the night. Although it was dark, he could see a little of her cocoa brown skin tone. He caressed her arms under the cover but not enough to wake her as the snoring continued uninterrupted.

He rolled over on his back and wondered what he would be doing now if he hadn't married Lisa.

Same as before.

Get a phone number, call to go out, three date rule and start the process again.

He was off that spinning wheel. His new reality was married and soon to be a father.

Lisa murmured in her sleep and rolled next to Doug. He felt her fingers gently brushing through the hairs on his chest. His hands were under his head and he smiled at the sensation running through his torso.

Much better than his three-date max.

***

The dishes were clanging noisily when Doug got up. Her side of the bed was empty and he wanted to be with her.

She was in a light grey jogging outfit with just enough baby bump stretching the grey T-shirt underneath. Her hair was pulled back in a ponytail. A small stack of silver dollar pancakes and sausages were on a plate.

"Good morning." He came behind her as she was finished washing the last dish. She turned her head to receive the incoming kiss on her neck.

"Good morning. Hungry?"

"Sure." He pulled out a couple of glasses and filled them with orange juice. He sat at the table and waited for her to join him.

"How did you sleep last night?" Lisa asked.

"Well." He sipped his orange juice.

"Liar." She offered him the plate with the pancakes on it.

"What do you mean?" he asked.

"Did you know that you have nightmares?"

"What?" Doug waved his hand and almost knocked over his juice. He quickly grabbed it from spilling over.

"At least twice a week. Something about that car accident. All I keep hearing is 'Please don't go.' You've got to talk about it with someone."

"Um," Doug hedged, "I'm sure it's nothing. Do you expect a big turnout for tryouts today?"

"Fine. Never mind." Lisa turned her head to the side once, acknowledging that he didn't want to talk about it. She poured the syrup over her pancakes. "Yes, I'm hoping for a big turnout. I have a few players that I'd like to pick up."

Doug reached for the Wall Street Journal and unfolded it to read the headlines. "I'm having lunch with Aunt Mona and may hit a few golf balls with Greg. I'll be home later this evening."

"What! You're not coming with me?" Lisa's fork stopped midstream as she was taking a bite of her pancake.

Doug lowered his paper. "No, I'm not. There will be several people there to help you. You keep saying I stifle you. So we'll try it your way." Doug took the last bite of sausage and rose from the table. He kissed Lisa on the forehead and went upstairs. He peeked out of the corner of his eye to see if she was following him.

Ten minutes later the motor started on her car and she was gone.

***

Lisa called her sister Terri on the way to the soccer field."

"Hi, baby sis. What's new in your world?"

"I'm going to soccer tryouts. Want to meet me there?"

Terri laughed, "No and tell my brother-in-law I said hello. I know he's sitting right next to you."

"No, I'm going alone. He's having lunch with Aunt Mona and hitting golf balls with Greg."

"What! If I were you, I'd turn that car around and follow his ass. This isn't normal for him."

Lisa reached a stoplight and waited for the green signal. She honked her horn to get the car moving in front of her. "I can't. I've got to pick my team for next year."

"Call him on your break. I'll meet you for lunch. Call when tryouts are over."

Lisa pulled into the parking lot next to one of her soccer players.

The girl waved and got out of the car, waiting for Lisa to follow.

"Hi Coach," she said. Under her arm was a light green soccer ball to compliment her shorts. Her dark hair was pulled away from her face in a ponytail.

"Hey, April. How are you?" Lisa opened the trunk of her car.

"I'll get that," April's father, Jack said with a smile. He took the bag of soccer balls for her "Where's Doug at? Is he feeling puny?"

Lisa laughed. "No, he's having lunch with his aunt. I'll see him later."

"Oh, okay. No worries. I'm staying for the whole thing. I'll carry the bag back to the car for you. Your husband will be upset if you lift anything heavy."

April had already run off to start practicing when Lisa turned to Jack. "Those balls aren't that heavy. I lift them all the time."

"Not now. I hope you aren't trying to lift these now." His eyes narrowed and his cheeks hardened with concern. "You're pregnant and have to take it easy."

"What is it with you Southern men? Pregnant doesn't mean invalid." His eyebrows rose and she sighed. "Fine. Carry the balls to the field. I need them at the first bench."

Jack hauled the bag onto his shoulder and walked away.

Lisa's phone rang and she answered. "Hello my handsome husband. Tryouts are about to start. I don't have a lot of time to talk."

"You really left me," he whined. "I thought you were going to beg me to come."

"Oh, not a chance. You gave me an out and I took it. Have fun with Mona. I'm having lunch with Terri so let's have dinner tonight at home and I want the biggest steak you can find."

"Red meat isn't good for—"

Click.

She dropped the phone in her tote bag and walked over to the bench with a smile.

Hopefully he got the hint.

***

"Ladies, thank you for coming to tryouts. The teams will be posted in the hallway of the rec center by Monday morning. Please enjoy your weekend." Lisa announced.

The girls gathered their gear and walked over to their parents.

"April," Lisa called out as she was leaving. "Please talk to me for a minute."

"Yes, Coach?"

"I know you as a player. This wasn't your best tryout. What's going on?"

Tears started flowing down the girls cheeks and she turned red as she tried to wipe them away. "It's Katie. We haven't heard from her since she left. I miss her."

"Sweetheart," Lisa bent to give April a hug, not knowing what else to do.

Mothering.

Don't panic.

She leaned back and brushed the tears away from the girl's face. "Is there anything I can do?"

"Find her."

Find her?

Of course, I can do that.

And I know the man who knows where to find her.

Lisa forced a smile to her lips. "I'll see what I can do."

April sniffed and ran past her dad.

He stared after her with a shake of his head but a smile for Lisa. "I'll grab that as promised."

"Jack, about Katie—"

"Leave it be, Coach. Everything's fine."

He picked up the bag and Lisa walked with him back to her car, not saying anything else.

***

"How was lunch with Mona?" Lisa asked.

Doug, who was in the laundry room washing when she came in, replied, "Great." He closed the lid of the washer. "How was lunch with Terri?"

"The usual," she said and placed her hands on the doorframe of the laundry room. "She and Ricky are still arguing."

"Shocking."

Lisa agreed with him on that one.

"How were tryouts?"

"Good. There were a couple of new girls that I'm considering adding to the team. Did you get my steak?"

He smiled. "Yes. I got the biggest prime rib that I could find. I'll cut it into thirty pieces and you can have three pieces per day over the next ten days."

"Not funny. I'm having ten pieces over three days. Did you start the grill? I'm hungry."

"Almost," he pulled her hand, "Come outside and sit with me."

Lisa followed his lead to the patio and watched him fire up the grill. She sat in a patio chair and began thinking about April's issue.

She knew Katie, Doug's old flame. Not who she would have wanted at her wedding, but that was in the past. Katie was Doug's past.

How was she going to ask him about her? Did she want to even if it would be for her player's welfare?

"What's the matter, Lisa?"

I may as well get this over with.

"It's April. You remember Jack and April, from the team, right? Apparently, your friend Katie was friends with their family and now has gone missing. April's worried about her."

"Oh." Doug moved back to the grill, hedging. He lifted the lid and picked up the fork to check the steak.

Lisa walked over to him and he avoided eye contact. "You know something, don't you?"

"Uh, yes, uh she's in Savannah." He stammered.

Lisa placed her hands on her hips and frowned. "Why?"

Doug looked at her and looked away. "Uh, her new job?"

A question? There's more and he's not telling me.

"Spill it Doug. I'm not stupid. You know more than you're telling."

Doug paused and let out a sigh. "I told her she was pregnant a few weeks ago. She made me promise not to tell anyone. She probably decided to have the baby in Savannah."

"PREGNANT! Who's baby!"

Doug threw his hands up to guard his chest. "How should I know? I know it's not mine and I didn't ask."

"Why the hell not? Are you sure? She called before we got engaged. Were you seeing her? Are you seeing her? Is that why you didn't want to come to soccer today?"

"No. I told you, it's not mine."

She knew that.

Why would she think that? She knew him. She trusted him.

Lisa turned away from the grill.

She remembered their honeymoon when he walked up to the hotel clerk and told her she was pregnant. She also remembered the Valentines party and Bambi's pregnancy. Add Jaylon's girlfriend Taquanda to the list.

It was starting to make sense and becoming a pattern.

"Did you walk up to her and tell her she was pregnant?"

Doug lowered his eyes.

"Douglas Arthur Bader."

"It just slipped out."

"No wonder she ran. You have to quit doing that. Women will be scared to talk to you."

"I know."

"Do you know how to find her?" Doug returned to the grill and stuck a fork in the steak. "It's medium rare. Please pass the plate. Oh, I have one right here."

Lisa snatched the fork from his hand. "Stop avoiding the question. Where the hell is she? April's upset and suspect Jack is too."

"Her father. He should know. He's part of the country club."

"Let's get them together." She grabbed his fork, pierced the steak on the plate, and chewed a bite. "Good."

"What? We're not getting involved."

"Oh yes we are. You just told me she's pregnant and it's not yours. She left town without a word. April's crying and Jack won't talk about it. You're not the only psychic. That's Jack's baby."

Lisa watched Doug take a step back from the grill and look far away into the distance. His lips pressed tight and his eyes turned upward. "You're right. It's most likely his."

She folded her arms across her chest. "What are you going to do?"

Doug sectioned off a couple of pieces of steak. He placed the morsel in between her lips. She savored the wood grilled taste spiced with her favorite seasonings.

"I'll make the call to Don Pennington and invite him out for drinks at Dupree. It's up to you to get Jack to show up. We'll leave the two of them to work it out."

Lisa wrapped her arms around his waist, raised her chin and looked in his eyes. "I knew you would know what to do."

Chapter 22

"Another one huh." Lisa said sleepily. "Good thing we're seeing Dr. Zwinger today. We've got to resolve this or I'll never get any sleep."

"How can you hear anything with the way you snore?" Doug rubbed his fingers through his hair and hoped the cold sweat that dripped from his body would calm down so that he could get the rest of his sleep.

"I hear everything."

"You don't. Now go back to sleep."

"How much sleep do you think I'm getting? Feel this." Lisa grabbed his hand and placed it on her abdomen. The baby began a rocking motion.

"Our baby will be running instead of crawling when he comes out." Doug smiled and nestled next to her.

"Or she." Lisa yawned. "She'll be playing soccer. Lots of soccer. I hope you're becoming a fan because when the World Cup is on, I'm worse than any guy watching a football game."

"The big screen TV is downstairs. I'll watch it with you and the rest of our seven kids."

"No. Don't start that again." She sat up in the bed and placed her swollen feet on the floor. "I'll never see my toes with that many kids."

He slid out of his side of the bed, rounded the baseboard and offered his arm to help her up. "We'll have fun. We'll get the stroller and do evening jogs."

She accepted the offer and pulled herself up by his forearm. "My jogging is at the soccer field. Your jogging is at the soccer field. You're the honorary assistant coach. Guess what. I'm signing you up to get your National F license for coaching."

"You're what" he stepped back to see the look on her face. Her beautiful eyes sparkled when she stared at him and the corners of her lips turned upward into a sly smile.

"Of course I'm signing you up. This is a soccer family. Both of us should coach our baby. Mom and dad."

Doug brushed his hand down her elbow to her fingers lifting them up to his lips. "Let's talk about that later and get through the diaper stage first."

***

"Hello Dr. Zwinger." Doug extended his hand and Lisa followed. She took a seat on the couch and Doug sat beside her.

"Good evening. How are you?" Dr. Zwinger said. "Todays' session we're going over concerns. Each of you will write one concern on this sheet of paper and give it me. Summarize it in one word. We will work on one or both during this session."

Doug and Lisa wrote their concerns down.

"Give this to you?"

"Yes, I'll give it back. Are you finished, Doug?"

"Yes."

The shrink held out his hand and Doug handed his concern over to the man.

"I see. Take a look." The doctor handed them back the papers.

Doug and Lisa both opened them.

"Secrets!" Lisa exclaimed. "Are you kidding me? You're the master of secrets, Doug!"

"Seriously, Lisa? I tell you everything."

"Like your nightmares?"

Doug crumpled the paper in his hand. "You wrote control freak. It's fair. We both know it."

"How are your actions *fair*?"

The doctor cleared his throat and Doug and Lisa turned to him. "How about I lead the discussion here?" They nodded halfheartedly. "Good. Let's discuss the secrets. Doug what concerns you about Lisa's secrets?"

Doug looked at her. "You're hiding your dating history and refuse to talk about it."

"Because it's not relevant." Lisa's folded her arms across her abdomen. "Let the dead be buried and that absolutely includes ex-boyfriends."

"You almost married that guy. It's relevant." He argued back. "I need to know these things."

"Why? It has nothing to do with us. All you need to know is I love you; I married you. I'm having your baby. No one else matters to me."

"So why can't you talk about it with me?" Doug asked.

"Probably the same reason why you won't talk about your nightmares about the car accident and parents with me. You haven't told me anything about your past relationship with your ex-fiancée and your nightmares about her are getting worse. The further along I get in this pregnancy we get, the more you have them."

"You're changing the subject," he answered.

"No, I'm not. You can't say secrets and then hedge when I bring up yours. Two-way street and I'm not discussing Jaylon just like you're not discussing your ex. What about your control issues? You've planned every day of my pregnancy. You insist on going almost everywhere with me. If you keep this up, we're not going to make it. I can't stand all of this control. I have my own life and you are a part of it."

Doug stood up and walked towards the window.

"Where are you going? I'm not finished with you?"

Dr. Zwinger held his hand up motioning for Lisa to be quiet.

Doug continued to look out of the window.

"Doug, how do you feel about Lisa's concerns?"

He turned slowly to look at Dr. Zwinger. "She is right that I'm unusually close. I'm protecting her and our baby."

"Why?"

Lisa wrestled to stand up from the couch and Doug rushed over to her and settled her back down. He looked her in her eyes. "I just can't let anything to happen to you."

Each word struck her core in loud resounding tones rushing through the tiniest of blood cells. It echoed in her heart and she wanted to know more. "Why, Doug? Nothing's going to happen to me. My obstetrician says I'm fine. The baby's fine."

Doug released her and stood up. He paced the floor from couch to window and back again.

Lisa looked to Dr. Zwinger for help. He remained calm and motioned for Lisa to sit, wait, ad give Doug a chance to answer.

"Lisa doesn't know this. Dr. Zwinger, you and I have had extensive talks on it." Doug sat down next to her, picked up her hand and held it, not meeting her gaze.

"I told you that my parents were killed when I was in college. They had another passenger in the car. My girlfriend, Tiffany. She didn't make it either. They did an autopsy. She was pregnant." Shaken, he forced the words out of his mouth to continue. "I think Tiffany was coming with my parents to tell me about the pregnancy but they never made it. I was in my dorm waiting for them to go to dinner when the state police came to my door. My entire world shattered in the blink of an eye. I had four burials within days of each other and one I never even knew about. A baby no one ever even knew about.

"Dr. Zwinger helped me to get through it. I channeled my energy strictly in the classroom. I went all the way through medical school. When I started my residency at a local hospital, a pregnant teenage girl was killed in an auto accident. She looked a lot like Tiffany" Lisa's eyes glistened and swelled with water.

"I wasn't sure if I could continue that career path. After my residency, I couldn't practice medicine anymore. I couldn't risk losing another life, so I went to law school. I didn't want anything to do with medicine so I became a divorce attorney."

He took in a deep breath and continued. "There was nothing that I could do to help Tiffany. She was gone before I even had a chance to help her, to know her, our baby. I've been unable to commit to anyone for years after that. I tried to make sure no woman could get close to me. I just couldn't go through that again. Losing something so precious to me again, not being there, able to help. I can't lose you like that, Lisa."

Lisa's lips parted on a breath. "Is this the real reason why you stay so close to me?"

"I love you. I can't lose you. Don't ask me to risk that. I can't."

Tears streamed down Lisa's face and she placed his head into her breasts. He felt her blouse dampen and realized that it was tears of his own. It had been years since he shed them and now it was time to let them go.

Doug felt a huge weight lift off his shoulders when he finally shared with Lisa his horrific past. He couldn't control what had happened to Tiffany and had to realize that Lisa and Tiffany had different paths. He would see and be with Lisa and their baby.

"Good, Doug. That's good. That's the biggest breakthrough we've had together in years. This is good. We'll set up another session but I want you two to really talk before then. Really talk. Open up. You love each other. Share."

Doug nodded. "Thank you, Doctor."

"It's my honor, Doug."

Chapter 23

Lisa closed her eyes and relaxed on the silent ride home. She was relieved to know the root cause of his controlling behavior. No wonder he was so obsessive about her and the baby. He'd lost his family in one fell swoop and a baby that he never got to know.

When they arrived home, Doug opened the door and stopped in the foyer. Lisa came in after him and headed toward the stairs. He stopped her, embraced her. "I'm sorry that I didn't tell you about this earlier."

She looked up into his eyes and saw the sadness and strain in his face. This was the first time that Doug shared his feelings on a deep personal level.

"It's okay. I think I understand now." She hugged him tightly, stroked her hands down his back. "Are you okay?"

"I am."

"Do you want me to make you some hot chocolate?"

He smiled weakly. "No, I'll do it."

He turned on the stove and filled the teakettle with water.

"I'll get the cups." Lisa reached for the clean cups in the dish rack and placed them on the table. She picked up the packets of instant hot chocolate and poured them in the mugs.

Doug poured the water and returned the kettle to the stove.

She stirred both cups and inhaled the chocolate treat garnished with the whip cream.

"This is good, Doug." She wasn't talking about the drink.

He knew that too.

"I know it's not easy for you, but I promise, I'm going to be fine."

"I know," he said softly. "I've just never forgotten and it will always be with me."

Lisa reached for his hand. "I can't and won't ask you to forget it. It's part of you but so am I. I'm not Tiffany. I want our marriage to work. We have to live each day as it comes but you can't think that I'll have the same outcome. I can't fix the past."

"That wasn't my—" He swallowed at the look in her eye. "I'll try. No promises or guarantees. But I'll try."

"And I'll try to be more understanding too. I love you, baby."

"I love you too."

Chapter 24

Doug slipped his cool fingers into her warm hand in the middle of the night. He soon released it and brushed his hand against her abdomen softly stroking but soon the soft skin rose with an elbow or knee crossing the palm of his hand.

Lisa lifted her hand and covered his while she shifted to satisfy their baby.

Doug chuckled at the baby's moves. "I didn't mean to wake you but it looks like someone else is awake too."

"That's okay. I couldn't sleep. I feel stretched to the limit."

"We have the party at Terri's house today. Do you feel up to going?"

"Oh yes, I wouldn't miss it. I know you won't leave my side."

"Lisa," he sighed.

"Yes?"

"We've known each other almost a year and you're still with me. I thought you would have packed up and moved out by now."

Lisa sleepily smiled with her eyes still closed, reached for his hand and placed it back on her abdomen. The baby stretched and Lisa leaned back into Doug hoping to give it some room.

"I love you. Of course I'm staying.

Lisa shoved the cover's down below her waist. Doug pulled them over to his side.

"Too warm?"

"Yes."

"There's pressure in all marriages. Ours is no different. Your past. My *race*. Secrets. We've had our problems. If you were any other man I would've walked out."

"And I would have followed you." He propped up the pillows so they could sit up and talk.

Lisa pushed herself back so she could get comfortable. She pulled his face into hers lightly touching his lips. "I know," she snickered. "I wouldn't need to tell you where I went. You'd just show up. We're unexplainably bonded."

"Yes we are. I've been thinking." He paused and she tensed. Last time he'd been *thinking,* she'd lost steak privileges for a month. "This planner has to be miserable for you."

Miserable?

One way of putting it.

"After the baby is born, we'll get your mother to watch the baby and go to the Brazilian Steak House and spend the weekend in downtown Atlanta. We'll do whatever you want. Our time alone."

A smile swept across her face. "Oh, I'd love that. I miss my red meat."

He snickered, "It's all you can eat and you know the rules."

She slapped his chest. "I won't be pregnant anymore silly."

"Breastfeeding."

"No way. Bottle. No babies hanging off my tit. I've got soccer players and parents. No exposure around them.

"Try it for a little while." He lifted her gown and placed his hand on her tender swollen breast. He covered his mouth over her nipples.

"Oh tender, stop." He lifted his head and said. "Good nourishment for the baby."

"There will be enough to do without adding breast feeding to the list. We'll be washing bottles, changing diapers and losing sleep. We're going to be parents." Doug laid his head beside her cheek. "We are. Our baby's coming soon."

***

"Let me get that."

Doug opened the car door and helped Lisa to her feet. Her hands and legs were swollen and she waited for Doug to retrieve the pecan pie from the back before she moved towards Terri's front door with Doug following behind.

Terri answered and gave Lisa a big hug. "Good thing your husband knows medicine. If you drop that baby in the middle of my party, I'm running."

They both laughed.

"How's my favorite sister-in-law?" Doug smiled and winked.

"Oh, I'm not your favorite. Come on in. Everyone's outside in the backyard."

"Where's Ricky?" Lisa asked.

Terri sighed. "Not here but will be later with his no-good friend bad-news Chris."

They followed Terri through the living room to the sliding glass door to the patio where several guests were gathered.

Lisa spotted her mother and hugged her.

"I believe today is the day," Ann exclaimed.

"I hope so," Doug said while patiently waiting his turn to hug his mother-in-law. "This has been a long pregnancy."

Lisa smacked his arm. "Shut up, Doug."

"Ow! Save that fight for later. You'll need the energy for the baby."

Lisa wiped her eyebrow, which was watering from the heat. "It's a little warm out for me. I'm going in the kitchen to sit after I speak to a few people."

"I'm going with you."

Lisa glared at Doug. "No, you're not. I'm not far away and if I need you then I'll have someone come and get you. Remember our talk. Personal space, personal space. We'll have our time together. I want to spend time with my family. Go talk to my dad. I think I hear him calling you."

"I get the hint. Mom, take care of her. Are you going inside with her?"

"Yes," she sighed. "I promise I'll take care of her. Shoo."

Lisa walked back inside the sliding glass doors.

Terri pointed her to a kitchen chair. "I want you to be comfortable. Sit."

"Sure."

"My first grandchild. This is so exciting. I can't wait to see my baby. Do you want me to get you anything?"

"I can't. I'm stuffed and I can barely move. I just want–" Lisa looked up and saw Terri followed by Doug.

He brought a large towel and a couple of pillows. "For you. Let me help you up." Doug helped lift her and slid the pillow and towel under her, propping one behind her back. "I know we'll be here for a while so I brought this for you."

"Thank you," she smiled

"Oh, you should lift your legs." Doug pulled over a kitchen stool and propped her feet up. "That should do it."

Terri shook her head. "It looks like you're getting a lot of attention. Enjoy it while you can."

"This is your niece or nephew. I want our baby to be healthy even if I must pamper Lisa."

Terri laughed. "I don't think Ricky would ever pamper me, pregnant or not. I hope you appreciate this, sis."

Lisa leaned forward while Doug stuffed a pillow behind her back. "I do, Terri. I'll miss being pampered. We both will be pampering the baby."

Doug fluffed the pillow. "I'll be outside. Back in thirty minutes."

"Well trained." Ann chuckled. "And I have no doubt that he'll be back in thirty minutes right down to the millisecond."

***

Doug came back into the kitchen and flashed a smile across the room at Lisa. She laughed as she caught his eye.

Ann turned and faced him. "I don't think that I'll get to see my own grandchild."

Doug laughed. "You will, I promise. Once I've had my turn."

"Dinner will be ready soon." Terri said.

"Good, I'm starved." Ricky and Chris walked into the room and Lisa tensed at their arrival.

Her brother-in-law met her gaze. "Damn girl. You look past due. Are you okay?"

"I'm fine." Lisa said.

"Where's that cracker? I know he's not far away." Ricky said half-joking and turned to his friend. "Let's go out back and see what's up."

Ricky moved through the kitchen followed by Chris. He didn't wait for Lisa to respond.

"He's a nut," Ann said. "Did you see how fast he ran out of the kitchen? Too many women."

"Do you want to call everyone in?" Terri asked. "The rolls have about five minutes left before they are ready."

"I'll do it." Lisa said as she tried to push herself up from the table. I've got to stretch my legs."

"Oh no you won't." Ann said. "I've got this."

She disappeared through the sliding glass door and Lisa sank back in her chair.

"I'm not an invalid. Just pregnant." Lisa said. "Ooh. Maybe I am." She stretched back in the chair as the baby put a foot on her rib.

"Do you want me to get you anything?" Terri asked.

"No, Doug will be here in a minute. He needs something to do."

Doug and other guests came into the kitchen and assembled for a prayer led by Ricky.

"Good food, good treats, thank God, let's eat. Short and sweet." Ricky motioned for the family to line up, take a plate and serve themselves around the dining room table. Most of the family ate outside at the tables designated for the guests.

"I'll bring something for you. Stay put."

Doug left to get her a plate and she watched everyone having a good time and discussing various subject.

Work, sports, movies and travel.

Lisa disappeared to the bathroom and came back to find Doug standing by her designated place at the table.

"Are you okay?" he asked. "If you were in there any longer, I would've come to get you."

"It's just the bathroom," Lisa said.

"You're close. Sometimes women mistake labor for bathroom urges."

"Whatever." Lisa sat down and looked at the food he offered. No red meat. One ear of corn and a glass of water. She might not be too hungry, but she wasn't letting him get away with that. "Where's the rest of it?"

"Only small things. You're too close. If you require anesthetic you may vomit and risk choking. I'm looking out for you."

She looked at the sincerity in Doug's eyes. She wasn't that hungry. When he left, she'd have someone bring her what she wanted. "Thank you for looking out for me sweetie. Stacy and I have a lot to talk about. Come back in thirty minutes," she smiled.

"Maybe fifteen," he kissed her cheek and walked out of the sliding door.

Chapter 25

"Over here," motioned Dave who as sitting on a patio chair near the grill.

"Yes, sir." Doug stood next to him instead of taking the empty chair.

"Are you going to eat?"

"I can't. I won't be here long. Lisa is due any day now and I believe today is it. I just don't know when."

"Have a rib. I insist." Dave lifted his plate and Doug took a bite.

"Oh, these are good." Doug sat down in the chair that Dave initially offered. While he was eating, his thoughts wandered to his concern for Lisa. Was she ready for all that would transpire in the next couple of hours or the next couple of days?

"I notice that you don't leave Lisa at all. Is there a reason why?" Dave asked breaking Doug's trance.

"I want to be there for her. She knows how I feel about her. I don't want anything to happen to her during the pregnancy that I don't know about. I have medical training and know the risks," he answered.

"Lisa indicated that there's more to the closeness between the two of you. I'm concerned, Doug. I want to make sure that you're not obsessed with my daughter. That can turn from a healthy relationship to a restraining order."

Doug greatly respected Dave and had often sought personal advice that a mature man could provide. Although Dave was more like a father than a father-in-law, Doug wasn't ready to share too much of his life prior to meeting Lisa with him yet. "I'm going through counseling for it and Lisa is supporting me."

"That's great Doug—"

"Lisa's in labor."

Doug almost toppled the table when Stacy shouted into the commotion on the patio.

He was up and running before she managed to get through the glass sliding door and make room for him to pass.

"Please everyone step back. Lisa, what happened?"

"My water broke."

"Alright, we're out of here. Up."

Lisa managed to rise from the table and he escorted her to the car. They pulled out of the driveway and were on their way to the hospital.

***

"We have a boy." She looked at Doug holding the baby next to the bed. He'd been wonderful, never complaining no matter how hard she squeezed his hand. She watched him holding their son, the way he cradled the baby in his arms, the love on his face, not just for their child as he turned and met her gaze.

"He's beautiful, Lisa."

A smile swept across her face.

The door to her room opened and the rest of her family came in with well wishes. Her mom hugged her first.

"How do you feel, baby?" Ann asked.

"Exhausted. Happy, but exhausted." Lisa said. "It's good to see everyone."

"So, his name is William Douglas Bader III?" Stacy asked.

"Yes, it is." Lisa answered. "We're keeping the family name. Doug said that I can name the next kid. After all of this I don't know about any more though."

Everyone laughed.

"I understand. Eight pounds and ten ounces is a huge baby to push out. I don't think I could do that." Terri said.

The family cooed as Doug passed the baby to his wife and Lisa held her son as everyone gathered close to look at the little guy.

Doug bent close to kiss his son's forehead, "I've waited a long time for you to get here."

Lisa smiled, "Not as long as I have."

Epilogue

"It's been quite a year." Lisa said while sitting on the bed pulling up her sheer pantyhose."

"It has." Doug answered. He splashed his favorite woodsy cologne on his neck.

"No more nightmares?" she asked and stepped into her red tea length cocktail gown. She held the loose dress and turned her back to him. "Zip me please."

He nodded and complied. "No more. Dr. Zwinger's been helpful with that. Douglas keeps us very busy so when I get a chance to rest, I take advantage of it."

"It's nice that Mona's allowing me to work part-time for a while. I don't like to admit it, but everything was getting overwhelming. I don't want to give up soccer to handle the baby and a full-time job."

"I don't want you to give up soccer either." He fastened the buckle on his black belt. "It's your passion. I'm becoming a fan because of you."

Lisa slipped on her heels and walked over to the dresser where Doug was standing. "How do I look, counselor?"

"Gorgeous. I love you in red. It should be your entire closet." Doug wrapped his arms around Lisa's waist and asked. "Are you ready?"

Lisa placed her fingers on his butt and squeezed. "I am and I love you too."

"Mark's estate isn't far from here. We should get there in about twenty minutes."

"Should I call Mona and check on Douglas before we leave?"

"No, he's fine. She's having great-nephew time. We'll pick him up in the morning. I want my night alone with my wife, and I mean all of it." He covered her lips and devoured the ruby lipstick.

She breathed a sigh as he let her up for air. "Let's skip the damn party. I've got new lingerie and I want to wear it...and then not wear it." She placed her ruby manicured nails on his lips and laughed when he nipped them.

"New lingerie?"

"Uh huh" She smiled and traced her fingers down his clean-shaven jaw line.

"*Cough, cough, ahem,* I do believe I'm coming down with cold."

"I believe so too counselor." She smiled and winked at him. "You should be in bed right away."

"Argh" he groaned. "We stay one hour then back home."

"Promise?"

"Promise."

ABOUT THE AUTHOR

MIA MAE LYNNE - has enjoyed writing from the time she was in grade school. She started a diary and wrote in the journal for seven years. She always knew that one day all her creative ideas would come into fruition and writing has been her escape.

"The Chronicles of Fate" series was born in the metro Atlanta area allowing her to explore her creative side. The series was later renamed to "Southern Men Don't Fall in Love" with "Atlanta's Most Eligible Bachelor" as the first book in the series with many more to follow. She has enjoyed writing the series and has embraced each of the characters as they have entrusted her with their stories to share with the world.

After discovering psychic and mediumship abilities, she became a student of spiritualism. She has newly begun this path and has explored the traditional areas of tarot, numerology, astrology and other related areas of interest in the metaphysical arts. She has received training from the Fellowship of the Spirit in New York as well as read numerous books and attended various classes to expand her knowledge.